SHE WAS THE
LADY IN ENGLA
UNHAPPY.

When a marriage of convenience made Margarita the
wife of Nicholas Beauchamp, she was the envy of every
beauty in the realm. Her bridegroom was both incredi-
bly handsome and the lord of one of England's most
splendid estates. In addition, his many female conquests
made no secret of his skill as a lover.

In short, this marvelous man offered Margarita everything a woman could want—except the one thing that
only an innocent as foolish as she would even dream of
asking for. The one thing that Nicholas Beauchamp refused to grant to any woman—his own true love. . . .

MARGARITA

About the Author

Joan Wolf is a native of New York City who
presently resides in Milford, Connecticut, with
her husband and two young children. She taught
high school English in New York for nine years
and took up writing when she retired to rear a
family. Her previous books, THE COUNTER-
FEIT MARRIAGE, A KIND OF HONOR, A
LONDON SEASON, A DIFFICULT TRUCE,
THE SCOTTISH LORD, and HIS LORD-
SHIP'S MISTRESS are also available in Signet
editions.

SIGNET REGENCY ROMANCE
COMING IN DECEMBER 1988

---•---

Anita Mills
Duel of Hearts

Amanda Scott
Lord Greyfalcon's Reward

Dorothy Mack
The Steadfast Heart

---•---

MARGARITA

By
Joan Wolf

A SIGNET BOOK

NEW AMERICAN LIBRARY

Copyright © 1982 by Joan Wolf

SIGNET TRADEMARK REG. U.S. PAT. OFF. AND FOREIGN COUNTRIES
REGISTERED TRADEMARK—MARCA REGISTRADA
HECHO EN CHICAGO, U.S.A.

SIGNET, SIGNET CLASSIC, MENTOR, ONYX, PLUME, MERIDIAN AND
NAL BOOKS are published by NAL PENGUIN INC.,
1633 Broadway, New York, New York 10019

First Printing, June, 1982

  4   5   6   7   8   9   10   11   12

PRINTED IN THE UNITED STATES OF AMERICA

CHAPTER ONE

O when her life was yet in bud,
   He too foretold the perfect rose.
             Tennyson

May, 1812

There was a letter for the earl from South America. The butler took it from the English naval captain who had brought it to the door of the Earl of Winslow's town house in Berkeley Square. "It is from his lordship's granddaughter," Captain Williams told the butler. "I promised her I would deliver it personally."

"His lordship is not at home at present, Captain, but I will see to it he gets the letter the moment he returns."

Captain Williams nodded. "I shall be at Obbetson's for a week or so if his lordship would care to see me."

The butler inclined his head. "Very good, sir. I shall inform his lordship."

"Thank you." Another nod and Captain Williams

1

was gone, leaving the surprising letter in the custody of Reid.

Reid had been butler to Lord Winslow for fifteen years now, and the events that made this letter so interesting had occurred long before he had arrived to serve the Beauchamp family, but, in the way of all servants, he was well acquainted with the past history of his employer. Thirty years ago Lord Winslow's only child, his daughter Mary, had defied her parents and married Don Antonio Vicente Carreño, a Venezuelan. She had gone off to Venezuela with him, and his lordship had since then refused to recognize her existence. The heir to the earldom was his brother's son, Nicholas Beauchamp, who was at present twenty-three years of age.

When the earl came in two hours later, he was in a good mood. He had just managed to beat the Regent out of a painting they had both been interested in, and he was feeling very pleased with himself. The letter from Venezuela came as a distinct shock.

"Who did you say brought it?" he asked his butler.

"A Captain Williams, my lord. He said he would be at Obbetson's should you require to speak to him."

The earl grunted, nodded dismissal, and very slowly began to open the letter. He knew he had a granddaughter and four grandsons. He had had his own way of finding out about the Carreño household in Caracas, although he had never once in thirty years had a direct communication from Mary. They both, it seemed, shared the family characteristic of unforgivingness. But this wasn't from Mary; it was from her daughter. He opened the letter and read:

San Pedro, April 1812

Dear Grandfather,

I take the liberty of writing to you at this time because I have news I think you should be put in possession of. My mother was killed in the earthquake of March 26. She was in the cathedral in Caracas when the roof collapsed. My brother Antonio, who was in the army barracks at the same time, was also killed.

I am asking Captain Williams, who is a friend of my father's, to carry this letter for me. I am sorry that it contains such unhappy news.

Your granddaughter,
Margarita Josefina Theresa
Carreño y Beauchamp

When the old man had finished the letter, he leaned his elbow on his desk and shaded his eyes. Mary dead. It did not seem possible. Fifteen minutes later he rang the bell and instructed Reid to have a message taken to Captain Williams.

* * *

The Earl of Winslow had an imposing presence, and Captain Williams found himself a little awed by the tall, upright, dignified old man. "I asked you to come visit me, Captain," the earl said crisply, "because I wish to discover more about the situation in

Venezuela. My granddaughter has written to tell me that my daughter was killed in an earthquake."

There was not a flicker of emotion on the aristocratic old face. Captain Williams said after a moment, "That is correct, my lord."

"I did not know there had been an earthquake. It was a bad one?"

"One of the worst," replied Captain Williams soberly. "Ten thousand were killed in Caracas alone."

"I understand my daughter was in the cathedral. She had become a Catholic then?"

"Yes, my lord. It was Holy Thursday afternoon. The cathedrals were filled all over Venezuela. There was a heavy loss of life in Valencia, Barquisimeto, Trujillo, and Mérida. My ship was anchored in the port of La Guaira, and in that whole city only three houses remained standing."

"It sounds very bad indeed." The earl's voice was even and strong, not the voice of an old man. "How did my granddaughter come to escape?"

"Margarita had a fever and Doña Maria insisted that she stay at home. Otherwise she too would have been in the cathedral."

"And my grandson was in the army barracks?"

"Yes, my lord. As you must know, two years ago Venezuela declared her independence from Spain. Antonio was a colonel in the Republican forces. The whole Carreño family is deeply Republican, and Don Antonio and the other boys were attending a meeting at the Bolívar house that afternoon. That is why they were not in the cathedral, and that is what saved their lives."

"I am aware of Venezuela's declaration, Captain. What I wish to discover is for how long the country is likely to remain independent."

Captain Williams sighed. "The tide is running out, I fear. The problem is that independence is the dream of the Creole aristocrats. The rest of the country—the pardos, the Indians—have no interest in national liberty. And the priests have started preaching that the earthquake was the vengeance of God on the country for turning its back on Spain. Miranda is in charge of the Republic, but his troops are raw and inexperienced. I doubt if he can hold out against Monteverde for much longer."

"This Monteverde is the general in charge of the Royalist forces?"

"Yes, my lord."

"What will happen to the Republicans if Spain wins?"

"God knows, my lord. This Monteverde is nothing but a noncommissioned naval officer who has been lucky enough to win a series of victories—thanks in part to the indecisiveness of General Miranda. He is not a man I should care to surrender to."

The earl stared for a moment at his still-shapely hands, lying quietly on his knees. Without looking up he said, "Tell me about my granddaughter."

"About Margarita?" The captain sounded surprised.

"Yes. You said you knew the whole family."

A strange, gentle smile came over the captain's face. "She is the loveliest child I have ever seen," he said softly.

5

The earl looked up. "How old is she?"

"Fifteen, my lord."

After a moment the earl spoke, slowly and deliberately. "Are you returning to Venezuela, Captain?"

"Yes, my lord. I have been given command of the gunboat *Revenge*."

"Will you carry a letter to Don Antonio for me?"

"Yes, my lord."

"If you would not mind waiting one moment, I will write it now."

"I don't mind waiting, my lord."

The old man inclined his head, moved to an elegant writing table and sat down. Captain Williams looked at the walls around him with awe. They were filled with paintings, and even his amateur eye recognized the work of masters like Titian, Rubens, and Rembrandt. The earl was rising from the table, letter in hand, when there was a sound of an angry voice in the hall, and the door flung open.

"I want to talk to you," the intruder said grimly to the Earl of Winslow.

"Yes, I rather thought you would," the earl returned suavely. "First, however, let me introduce you to Captain Williams, who has brought me news from Venezuela. My nephew, Captain, Mr. Nicholas Beauchamp."

Nicholas hesitated a moment, then he came across the room to the captain, his hand held out. "How do you do, Captain. I'm sorry, I didn't realize there was anyone with my uncle."

Captain Williams found himself looking at one of the most sensationally handsome young men he had ever seen. But, although Nicholas Beauchamp's voice had been cordial, there still remained a line between his brows that spoke eloquently of temper. "That is quite all right, Mr. Beauchamp," he replied quietly. "I was on the point of leaving."

"Captain Williams has brought me a letter from your Cousin Margarita, Nicholas." The earl's voice was level and emotionless. "My daughter Mary is dead."

There was a startled pause. "Oh," said Nicholas Beauchamp. Then, belatedly, "I'm sorry, sir."

The earl inclined his head. "I thank you, Captain, for your good offices," he said to Captain Williams's stoic face. He crossed the room and handed Williams the letter.

"I am happy to be of service, my lord," the captain returned woodenly and, with considerable relief, turned and left the room.

* * *

He dined that evening with some friends who moved in the lower echelons of London society, and he asked them curiously if they knew anything about the Beauchamp family.

"I have never met them, Ned," returned his friend Mr. Embleton, "but there are few people in London who don't know about the earl."

"Well *I* met him. This afternoon. A cold fish if ever I saw one." Captain Williams looked disgusted.

"He's tremendously aristocratic, I understand. Even the prince stands a bit in awe of him."

Captain Williams helped himself to a draught of wine. "Well, that young nephew of his don't seem to be in awe of him. He was spoiling for a fight and wasn't at all pleased to be interrupted by my inconvenient presence."

"Oh, Nicholas. Him at least I've seen. He broke Murray's driving record from London to Newmarket last year. Bested it by half an hour. There's been talk about him ever since he got sent down from Oxford. He's a wild one all right."

Captain Williams raised his eyebrows. "He seems rather young for such celebrity."

"I sat next to him once at a mill," put in Mr. Fergus, the youngest member of their company. "He's a good sort, I thought. The gossip is that he and Lord Winslow are at drawn daggers over money. The earl is a great collector, and the story goes that he's bankrupting Winslow in order to buy paintings. Nicholas don't like that—after all, Winslow's his inheritance. He's been fighting with his uncle for years to put money into the estate, but the old man refuses. Nicholas ain't *his* son, after all, or even his grandson."

"He's his great-nephew?"

"His nephew," said Mr. Embleton positively. "Nicholas's father was the earl's son by a second marriage. Christopher was almost twenty years younger than the present earl."

"Christopher Beauchamp. Do you mean *Captain* Lord Christopher Beauchamp, the one who was killed in the Battle of the Nile?"

"The same. A navy man like yourself."

8

Captain Williams smiled ruefully. "Hardly like myself. He was on his way to a brilliant career."

"Well the Frenchies put a stop to that. That left Nicholas as the only heir. The earl never had children."

Captain Williams finished his wine. "On the contrary, he had a daughter. She married a Venezuelan gentleman years ago. She was a very lovely lady, the pick of a bad lot, I'd say."

"Was?" inquired Mr. Fergus.

"Yes. She was killed in the earthquake two months ago."

"Oh. I say, is that why you went to see the earl?"

"Yes. I brought him the news. He didn't bat an eyelash."

Later, in his bed at Obbetson's, Captain Williams lay thinking of all he had learned that day. Then he thought of the warm and loving Carreño family in Caracas. Mary had had to turn her back on her country, her family, and her religion when she had married Don Antonio, but there was no doubt at all in Captain Williams's mind that she had made the right decision.

CHAPTER TWO

All red with blood the whirling river flows.
Matthew Arnold

It was a little more than two years later when Captain Williams called once again at the Earl of Winslow's house in Berkeley Square. He had arrived in England four days earlier, and after reporting to the Admiralty, the very next person he had called to see was the earl. This time he was fortunate enough to find his lordship at home. Reid ushered him into the library where the earl was sitting, waiting for him.

"Ah, Captain, how good to see you. May I offer you a glass of Madeira?"

"No, thank you, my lord. As you may suppose, I am here once again to bring you news from Venezuela."

"Please sit down, Captain." The old man gestured regally toward a chair, and when Captain Williams was seated he continued. "When last I saw you I gave you a message to deliver to Don Antonio Carreño. He did not choose to answer it. Am I to assume he is replying now?"

"My visit pertains to your granddaughter, my lord, if that is what you mean."

The earl carefully put his hands together. "I wrote Don Antonio two years ago that war was for men and that he should send his daughter to me. He chose not to do so. He has now changed his mind?"

"I don't know, my lord. He is dead."

"I see." The earl studiously regarded his hands. "Perhaps you had better tell me the whole."

"Venezuela is in ruins, my lord, and the Carreño family has shared its fortunes. Antonio, as you know, was killed in the earthquake two years ago along with his mother. Andrés, the third son, was killed in May at the Battle of Carabobo. A month later Ramón fell at La Puerta. It was then, in June, that I went to Caracas to beg Margarita to come back to England with me. I knew from Don Antonio of your invitation, you see."

"And?"

"She would not come, my lord. Valencia was under heavy siege from Boves, the Royalist leader, and Don Antonio was in command of the town. She refused to leave without her father."

"But you said he was dead?" The earl's voice for once was harsh with feeling.

"Yes, my lord. Valencia fell on July 9. Boves turned his troops on the city." He looked somberly at the earl. "Have you ever heard of the *llaneros*, my lord?"

"No, Captain."

"They are horsemen who live on the *llanos*—the grassy plains around the Orinoco River in the east of Venezuela. They are half-naked savages who kill for the pleasure of it. Boves has raised them for Spain, promising loot as their reward. Rape, torture, and mutilations follow in their wake. They lanced or knifed both the soliders and civilians who had withstood their siege in Valencia. I have heard that Boves personally lanced to death Don Antonio Carreño."

"Dear God, Captain," said the earl, his strongly marked brows drawn together. "What kind of a country is Venezuela?"

"A country that is bleeding to death, my lord."

"Then why did you leave my granddaughter there?" the old man demanded harshly.

"I said Valencia fell on July 9, my lord. On July 6 Simón Bolívar evacuated Caracas. When I arrived in the city from La Guaira, it was virtually deserted. Twenty thousand people had decided to go with Bolívar rather than wait for Boves."

The earl had long since raised his eyes from his hands and was now regarding Captain Williams steadily. "Evacuated?" he asked. "Where did they go?"

"I understand they were heading for the coast, my lord. They had not been heard of when I had to leave for England."

"And my granddaughter was with them?"

"Yes, my lord. Thank God her brother Fernando was with her. And Bolívar is a cousin of the Carreños. He will take care of Margarita, if he can."

"Was this Boves in pursuit?"

"It is not so much Boves they have to fear at present as the climate. They have left the mountains, my lord, and it is the rainy season. Fever will be their biggest foe."

There was a tiny pause, then the old man leaned forward in his chair, his eyes commanding the attention of Captain Williams. "*I want my granddaughter*, Captain Williams. She is all that is left of me in this world, and I want her here. In England. Do you understand me?"

"Perfectly, my lord."

"Do you return to South America?"

"I do not think immediately, my lord."

"Prepare to embark, Captain," the earl said grimly. "I still count for something in this country. I will speak to Yorke at the Admiralty. I want you to find my granddaughter and I want you to bring her to England. You may bring her brother, too, if he will come."

"I doubt if Fernando will come, my lord," Captain Williams answered with sober deliberateness. "But if Margarita is alive I shall bring her, you may rest assured of that."

* * *

Six weeks later Captain Williams was sailing into the port of La Guaira. He stood on the deck of his ship and watched the deceptively peaceful sight before him. Mountains plunged straight into the sea from heights of seven thousand feet. The water around the ship was green and blue and violet. Porpoises played in the sparkling sea, and gulls circled slowly and gracefully. Next to the ship a flying fish leaped out of the water in a shimmering shower of light. It did not seem possible that war could exist in such an enchanted place.

The news Captain Williams learned at La Guaira was not good. On August 18 Bolívar had tried to make a stand against Morales at Aragua de Barcelona, on the coast. He had had three thousand men against Morales's eight thousand. Morales had prevailed and, disciple of Boves that he was, had cut the throats not only of all the prisoners but also of a large part of the inhabitants, as well as a large number of refugees from Caracas. He had even, Captain Williams's informant told him, carried the massacre into the parish church, killing more than a thousand people who had sought sanctuary. Bolívar had subsequently fallen out with his captains Ribas and Piar and had been forced to flee to Cartagena. The refugees from Caracas had dragged themselves to Cumaná, where they were now, awaiting transportation to Margarita Island, the last Republican stronghold. Hours after he heard this news, Captain Williams set sail from La Guaira for the port of Cumaná, two hundred and fifty miles east.

* * *

The sun had come out at last and beat warmly down on the deck of His Majesty's gunboat *Revenge*. Captain Williams looked at the small, solitary figure standing so quietly by the rail, hesitated, then slowly approached it. "I hope you are warmer, Margarita, now that the sun is out," he said gently.

The girl, who was clad in a man's cloak, turned to look up at him. "It feels good on my face," she said in reply, and he came to stand next to her at the rail. He looked for a moment in silence at her hand as it rested on the rail, and he thought that although it was still too thin, at least it did not look like a skeleton's hand anymore. After a few days of seasickness, she had started eating, thank God, and even the uninteresting ship's fare had put some flesh back on her bones.

Captain Williams still found it difficult to recognize in this silent, impassive girl the sweet and lovely child he had known two years ago in Caracas. She had not given him any trouble about coming. When he found her at Cumaná she was with Doña Eleña de Mora, one of the few survivors of the evacuation march. Of all the twenty thousand Caraqueños who had left with Bolívar, only a few thousand were left. Margarita told him, with no expression in her voice, that Fernando had been killed at Aragua de Barcelona. Doña Eleña was the one who told him that Margarita had spent hours searching the battlefield for his body, refusing to leave him, if wounded, for the *llaneros'* spears. She had found him, and he was dead.

She had no clothes but the thin dress she was

wearing, and after they were out in the Atlantic a few days, Captain Williams gave her clean sailor's clothes to wear and his own cloak to wrap herself in for warmth. She had accepted both with the unquestioning passivity that he found so disturbing.

"When will we reach England, Captain Williams?" she asked him now.

"In a week or so, I should say. Your grandfather will be very pleased to see you, Margarita."

"It was kind of him to send you for me," she replied politely.

"He has been very worried about you."

"Yes. My father asked me if I wanted to go to England after my mother died. My grandfather had written to ask him if I might go. Of course I could not leave my family."

There was a bleak pause as they both realized once again that she no longer had any family to leave. "You will like England, I think," he said at last, gently.

"Yes." For a moment the huge dark eyes looked at him. "It hardly matters, now, where I go."

Captain Williams looked back into those eyes and realized that there was nothing he could find to say. So he put his large, warm hand over her small, cold one for a moment, then turned and left her to the solitude she so clearly preferred.

* * *

They arrived in England precisely ten days later, and Captain Williams brought Margarita, wearing her thin dress under his cloak, to the Winslow town house in Berkeley Square. The Earl of Winslow was clearly pleased to see his granddaughter. He had summoned a widowed cousin to Berkeley Square to act as her chaperone and guide, and Margarita had been consigned, with kindly concern, to the gentle ministrations of this lady. The earl then thanked the captain in measured tones, listened without comment to his report of the death of Fernando, and dismissed him with promises of mentioning his satisfaction to First Admiral Yorke at the Admiralty. Of Nicholas Beauchamp there had been no sign.

Captain Williams did not know why he felt such uneasiness over leaving Margarita. The earl would certainly take good care of her. Had he not called her "all that is left of me in this world." The captain wondered, and not for the first time, where that left his nephew. And he wondered again why it was his grand*daughter* the earl had been so anxious to see and not his grandsons.

CHAPTER THREE

Deep as first love, and wild with all regret;
O Death in Life, the days that are no more!
                                    Tennyson

December, 1814

The Earl of Winslow, Lady Moreton, his cousin, and
Margarita Carreño, his granddaughter, were seated
in the dining room at Berkeley Square having dinner. "We will be going down to Winslow for Christmas, my dear," the earl told his granddaughter. "A
few weeks in the country will do you good, although
I am pleased to see that your looks have already improved considerably since your arrival." He frowned
a little. "However, you are still far too thin. Eat your
dinner, my dear. Don't pick at it."

"Yes, grandfather," Margarita said docilely and put
some food in her mouth. The earl smiled at her approvingly. He was very pleased with Margarita. For
one thing, she spoke English beautifully. The earl
had been afraid she would have a disfiguring accent,
but her mother had seen to it that she spoke with

correct, English upper-class diction. The only indication she gave that English was not her native language was the formality of her style and an occasional tendency to slightly emphasize the last syllable in a word.

The earl was also pleased with her appearance. She looked like a half-starved kitten when she first arrived, but several weeks of good food and a new wardrobe had done wonders. She did not look English, but even the earl had to admit that she was lovely.

"When will we be leaving for Winslow, my lord?" It was Lady Moreton speaking. It had taken her a few minutes to get over her surprise. The earl, as far as she knew, hadn't set foot in Winslow since his wife died, and that was at least twelve years ago. He had, tacitly, already ceded it to his nephew. Lady Moreton wondered how Nicholas felt about his uncle's proposed visit. And she wondered, also, how Nicholas felt about the sudden arrival of this cousin from South America. If she knew Nicholas at all, and she did, a little, Lady Moreton thought that he would not like it.

They left for Winslow at the end of the week. The earl always traveled in a large, old-fashioned coach, emblazoned with his crest. There were a coachman and footman on the box and two footmen behind. Inside the carriage, dressed in a black pelisse of fashionable cut, her hands thrust into a warm chinchilla muff, Margarita sat with the Earl of Winslow and Lady Moreton. It was her first glimpse of the English countryside, and she gazed out of the window with mild interest. The bleak, cold, colorless land seemed to her very satisfactory, its leaden deadness preferable to the warmth and color of tropical Venezuela. It was easier not to feel in such a landscape as this. "Winslow is in Worcestershire, is that correct, grandfather?" she asked after a while.

"That is right, Margarita," Lord Winslow responded. "Winslow is one of the oldest sites in England. It is mentioned in *Domesday Book.*"

"*Domesday Book?*" she inquired, a slight pucker between her straight, dark brows. "Please, what is the *Domesday Book?*"

Lord Winslow stared at her. "You don't know?"

"No," said Margarita finally, and her small chin elevated a trifle.

"It was a tax survey made for William the Conqueror, my dear," said Lady Moreton calmly. "It listed all the major holdings in the country. Winslow is one of the few places mentioned that is still held by the same family."

" 'Roger of Beauchamp holds Winslow and there is his castle.' That was written in 1086, my dear child, and there are still Beauchamps at Winslow." The earl sounded complacent. "For you it should be a coming home."

Lady Moreton glanced quickly at him, then turned her eyes to the window. She thought of the Beauchamp who was waiting for them at Winslow now, and she frowned. She was not looking forward to this Christmas holiday. Nicholas and his uncle mixed about as well as oil and water, and she had a feeling that Margarita would only prove to be an irritant to Nicholas's already-precarious temper.

They were perhaps ten minutes from Winslow when the accident happened. The road had narrowed and there was a sharp turn. The phaeton coming so swiftly toward them had evidently not realized the coach was just around the curve. Margarita was turned toward her grandfather, listening to what he was saying, when suddenly the coach rocked violently. There was the sound of shouting. The earl reached out for her but she was pitched violently sidewards, her head struck the side of the coach, and she lost consciousness.

* * *

When she woke, she was lying in an enormous four-poster bed in a large room with a carved wooden ceiling. There was a fire roaring in the fireplace. Her head ached and she raised a hand to her forehead. There was no bandage. She closed her eyes for a minute and memory returned. The rocking coach. The shouting. There had been an accident. "Grandfather," she said out loud. "Where is grandfather?" Slowly she pushed back the covers. She was wearing a nightgown that she recognized dazedly as one of her own. She slid her legs off the side of the bed. She wasn't thinking clearly, only that she must get dressed and go find her grandfather. There was a wardrobe on the far side of the room. Her dress must be in there. Her feet touched the floor and she stood up. She took two steps forward, but a sudden on-slaught of dizziness caused her to cry out and grab for the nearest post of the bed, clinging to it while she tried to clear her head.

The door opened and a man's voice said, "You're awake! Where is Lucy? You shouldn't be out of bed."

She looked up, still holding to the bedpost. "My grandfather?" she asked. "Where is my grandfather?"

The man came into the room. "He's here," he said. "You're at Winslow. Get back into bed, please, before you faint." There was a pause. "I'm your Cousin Nicholas."

He seemed enormous. She raised her eyes to his face. It was unsmiling, and the eyes that were watching her steadily held no hint of sympathy. "Is he all right?" she asked.

There was a brief silence as he watched her, measuringly. She did not care for his look and let go of the post, standing up straight, unconscious of her nightgown and loose hair. "You can tell me the truth," she said firmly. "Is he badly hurt?"

Nicholas hesitated, but her eyes on him never wavered. "He's dead," Nicholas said. "It wasn't the accident itself that injured him, but the shock of it was too much for his heart. He was, after all, an old man." He came no closer to her. "Get back into bed," he repeated. "You have a concussion. You shouldn't have been left alone. I'll send Cousin Lucy to you."

She didn't answer but obediently turned toward

the bed. He was putting his hand on the doorknob when he glanced back, briefly. He was just in time to see her pitch forward, soundlessly, to the carpeted floor. He swore and moved quickly to bend over her. Her eyes were closed, the dark lashes lying still on too-pale cheeks. He bent and picked her up. She weighed hardly more than a child, but he knew that already. He had been the one to carry her upstairs. He put her carefully on the bed and pulled the covers over her, then he went to fetch Lady Moreton.

* * *

They wouldn't allow her to attend the funeral. She had been unconscious for almost eight hours and the doctor insisted that she stay in bed for a few days. When she was allowed up she was very quiet, keeping mostly to her room. Lady Moreton was very kind. Nicholas she hardly saw, except at dinner. She was painfully aware of him when he did appear. He was so large; she was not used to men as big as he was. He spoke quietly enough to her, but there was an atmosphere of contained force about him that made her shy away. It was there in the hard, arrogant line of cheek and jaw, in the graceful, catlike way he moved. In a way she could not explain, she felt he threatened her. But she was also painfully aware that Winslow now belonged to him and that she was there as his uninvited guest.

Those days of almost complete solitude gave her an uncomfortable amount of time to think. Her grandfather, the only anchor left in her life, was gone. She had no clue as to what would happen to her next. All her life Margarita had been surrounded by wealth and the security of a family who loved her. She now faced the fact that she was penniless, dependent on the good will of relations whom she did not know. She worried about the future but no coherent thoughts would come. The problem, she realized dully, was that she did not greatly care what happened to her. There was a frozen sea inside her where once there had been warmth and laughter and love. She ate, she talked, she answered questions, but it was only the outside shell of her that acted. The core was dead.

*　*　*

Five days after the funeral, the earl's lawyer arrived from London. Nicholas, the new earl, had awaited his coming with considerable apprehension. He knew that Winslow was his; it was entailed, there was no choice involved in its disposal. But the means to run Winslow, to bring it back from the neglect of too many years, of this he was not sure.

There had been no love lost between Nicholas Beauchamp and his uncle. Nicholas had been conscious all his life that the earl resented him, resented that it was Christopher's son and not his own who would inherit Winslow. Christopher was home only rarely, and the earl stood to Nicholas in the position of a father, but they never got along. Lord Winslow had not liked Nicholas's mother, either. He could not forget that her father's money came from manufacture, even though he was glad enough to see Christopher spend it. When she ran away with the young historian John Hamilton, who had been doing research at Winslow, the earl had felt justified in his opinion of her.

The earl's insatiable buying of art had been a subtle way to punish him, of that Nicholas was sure. The money that he took out of Winslow he put into his own private collection—a collection that was now world-famous, and which the earl was able to leave as he chose. Nicholas had always been fairly certain that some of the collection at least would be left to him: enough of it, at any rate, for him to put Winslow back on its feet again. But that was before the arrival of Margarita Carreño.

The Beauchamp family had been stunned by the welcome the earl had accorded to Margarita. His determined silence on the subject of his daughter had convinced everyone that he would have nothing more to do with her or anything that belonged to her. But Nicholas had not been so surprised. He never spoke of his mother either, but that did not mean he had forgotten. He feared that the earl might have decided that his own granddaughter would be a worthier recipient of the Winslow Collection than his graceless nephew. The earl had been under no illusions as to what Nicholas would do with the collection once he got his hands on it.

Mr. Francis Sheridan, the earl's lawyer, did nothing to put his mind at rest. After shaking hands and accepting a Madeira, he said, "Miss Carreño is still here, is she not, my lord?"

Nicholas still found the new title startling, but now he hardly noticed it. "Yes. She took a severe blow on the head during the accident. I haven't seen much of her, but she appears to be recovered."

"Good." Mr. Sheridan studiously avoided Nicholas's eyes. "I think she should be present for the reading of your uncle's will," he said quietly.

There was a pause, then Nicholas answered bleakly, "I see. I'll have her sent for."

When Margarita entered the room ten minutes later the two men were standing by the fire, staring down into the flames. There was silence in the room, and they both turned as the door opened and she came in, followed by Lady Moreton. Her cousin offered her a chair, and as she seated herself Mr. Sheridan looked curiously at the girl whose arrival had caused such consternation in the Beauchamp family circle. He saw a small face with skin the color of warm ivory. Her eyes were enormous, brown, and set slightly slantwise under dark, level brows. The nose was small and straight, the mouth surprisingly wide and full. She was lovely, he thought, and very young. "Thank you for coming down, Miss Carreño," he said. "I am about to read your grandfather's will, and as it concerns you, it will be best if you are present."

The grave, dark eyes widened a little in surprise. "Concerns me?" she asked. Her voice was very low, but clear and unaccented.

"Shall I go?" asked Lady Moreton.

"You may as well stay, Lucy," Nicholas said tautly. "The contents will hardly remain a secret for long." He gestured toward Mr. Sheridan. "Get on with it, then."

"Yes, my lord," the lawyer replied calmly, and he took up the papers he had spread out on the desk.

CHAPTER FOUR

My scheme was worth attempting: and bears fruit,
Gives you a husband and a noble name,
A palace and no end of pleasant things.
                                    Robert Browning

Fifteen minutes later he was still reading. The minor details, the bequests to old retainers, had all been taken care of. Mr. Sheridan cleared his throat and said quietly, "This next is what you will be interested in, my lord. 'I give devise and bequeath my entire art collection, the catalogue of which is attached to this document, to my nephew Nicholas Alexander George Beauchamp.'" There was a movement by the fireplace, and Mr. Sheridan looked up to meet Nicholas's suddenly brilliant eyes. "There is a condition, my lord. Your uncle added it only a month ago."

Nicholas's eyes narrowed. "And what is the condition, Mr. Sheridan?"

The lawyer looked back at the document. "'This bequest is made on the condition that the said Nicholas Alexander George Beauchamp marry my granddaughter Margarita Josefina Theresa Carreño within two weeks of the reading of this will.' "

"What!" It was Lady Moreton's voice. "You must be joking. Even Lord Winslow would not be as absurdly autocratic as that."

Mr. Sheridan was looking at the new earl. Nicholas's nostrils were pinched and there was a white line around his mouth. He gave a bitter little laugh. "On the contrary, it is exactly like him."

"I tried to convince him to change his mind, my lord. There is more than enough to provide for the both of you without necessitating this—arrangement. But you know how he was." The lawyer sighed. "If you don't agree to the condition, the collection is to go to the state."

"The will is legal?" asked Nicholas.

"It is legal, my lord."

There was silence as three pairs of eyes turned, as of one accord, to the small figure sitting so silently in the large armchair. Margarita's face, still and shuttered, gave away nothing. The lawyer thought suddenly that no girl of seventeen ought to be able to look like that. She turned her eyes toward Nicholas. "Do you need the collection?" she asked simply.

His mouth set in a hard, unpleasant line. "I need the collection. Winslow has been bled dry." His eyes, gray-green as a forest pond on a cloudy day, were steady on her face. "It appears it will be up to you, Cousin, whether I get it or not."

"You would be willing, then, to marry me?" Her

low, clear, precise voice expressed nothing but polite interest.

A muscle jumped in Nicholas's jaw. "Yes," he said. "I would."

"I see." She rose to her feet and said, with a lovely dignity, "I shall have to think about this. May I let you know my answer tomorrow?"

She had spoken to the lawyer and he nodded hastily. "Of course, Miss Carreño."

She nodded to him gravely and walked to the door, which Nicholas was holding for her. She stopped for a moment and looked up at him, a long, clear look. "I will tell you tomorrow," she repeated.

"Yes," he said evenly. "I heard you."

Lady Moreton stood silently watching them. She thought Margarita looked very small and helpless next to Nicholas's great height. The top of her head did not quite come to his shoulder. But the slim back was as straight as a ramrod, the head held proudly on its long slender neck. She passed out of the room with the grace and dignity one usually saw only in older women. Lady Moreton waited until the door was closed to ask Nicholas, "Would you really marry that child?"

"I don't have any choice, do I, Lucy? Nor does she, really, as I hope you will make clear to her. I may need that damn collection but so does she. Unless she brought money with her from South America?" Lady Moreton shook her head and he shrugged. "She has nothing, then. If she marries me, she will have money and position and a permanent home. Make her understand that, will you?"

Lady Moreton stood for a minute looking at the face of her younger cousin. It was a startlingly handsome face, with unusual gray-green eyes that were cool and deep and hard to see into. His brows and lashes were brown as was his thick, straight hair. That hair was the only boyish thing about Nicholas. His nose was high-bridged and imperious, his mouth beautifully shaped but with a look of ruthlessness about it that was very evident at the moment. He looked at present just what he was, a very intimidating young man in a temper. "Why on earth did he do it?" Lady Moreton asked him slowly.

He smiled. "He wanted his granddaughter here at Winslow," he said. "He always regarded me as an interloper."

His voice was perfectly pleasant, but Lady Moreton found herself saying hurriedly, "That's not true, Nicholas."

He shrugged. "Why he did it is not of importance at the moment, Lucy."

"No, I suppose not." She walked to the door. "I'll speak to Margarita."

*   *   *

What Lady Moreton had to say was little more than what Margarita had deduced for herself. Lady Moreton's representations were only echoes of Margarita's own Spanish logic, her impregnable sense of what she called *la realidad*. She had no choice. She must marry Nicholas Beauchamp.

What she didn't say to Lady Moreton, what she

would never admit to anyone, was that she was afraid of him. He did not want her, of that she was certain. And he was too big, too forceful. Life would never be too much for him. His kind of tough competence would deal with anything—even her. He was dealing with her already, as Lady Moreton's visit demonstrated. And she did not want to be dealt with. She wanted to be left alone. But she had to live somewhere. That was *la realidad*. And he needed the art collection. The following morning she told Nicholas Beauchamp that she would marry him.

* * *

It was not a happy wedding. At Margarita's insistence it was performed by a Catholic priest. Lady Moreton had been slightly shocked, but Nicholas had not cared.

They were married in the late afternoon with Lady Moreton and Sir Henry Hopkins acting as witnesses. Sir Henry was the owner of Twinings, a lovely Elizabethan manor not far from Winslow. He and his wife and Lady Moreton sat down to dinner with the newly married pair, a dinner that was not as awkward as it might have been under the circumstances. Margarita had the rigid Spanish sense of etiquette, and as hostess she rigorously subdued her own very real apprehensions and concentrated on her guests.

Those guests had the tact to leave early, and Lady Moreton too excused herself. She felt a pang of pity as she left Margarita alone in the drawing room with Nicholas, but there was nothing she could do to help the child now.

The two remained in silence for a full minute, then Margarita, seated in a wing chair by the fire, raised her eyes to where he stood by the chimney piece. "What do you want me to do?" she asked simply.

He looked at her for a moment before he answered, his eyes inscrutable. "Your things have been moved to the yellow room," he said, referring to the bedroom that adjoined the earl's, which was now his own. "Go upstairs and get into bed and wait for me."

Nicholas stayed where he was, his eyes on the empty door. He was angry about this marriage, and although he knew his anger should not be directed toward Margarita, he could not help some of it spilling over onto her. It was not that Nicholas had ever cherished romantic notions about marriage. He was himself the product of a notably unsuccessful union, and the breakup of his parents' marriage had left scars that were still not healed over. His father, a dashing twenty-eight-year-old naval hero, had married Charlotte Holt, a seventeen-year-old heiress whose family was of the city not the country. He had brought her to Winslow, got her with child, and gone back to sea. He appeared again from time to time, when he needed money to furnish a new ship, but for the most part Charlotte had been left to the companionship of Christopher's elder brother, the earl, and his unbending, censorious wife.

She stuck it out for eleven years and then, having

fallen deeply in love with the gentle, scholarly John Hamilton, she eloped with him. Two years later, after Christopher's death at the Battle of the Nile, they married.

Nicholas was devastated by his mother's elopement. All through his childhood she had been the sun around which his life revolved. He had loved her with the fierce devotion only a child can give. The letter she left him he did not understand. He only knew that she had deserted him, and he had been left with emotions of bitterness, pain, and heart-scalding hurt.

He never allowed himself to trust a woman again. He accepted the fact that he must marry some day, but he was not yet prepared to have anyone in so intimate a relationship with him that she could by rights push herself into his own fenced and guarded world. He was furious with his uncle for forcing this girl on him, and he was, unfairly, furious at Margarita as well.

He glanced at the clock on the table, put down the poker he had been holding, and walked with his distinctive, catlike stride to the door.

* * *

For Margarita too, it was the wrong time for marriage. The brutality of the last year had battered and drained her until every physical feeling in her was dead. Even had she been going to a man she loved, she would not have been able to respond. The wellspring of feeling in her had dried up.

The only emotion she felt, as she watched the door open and Nicholas come in, was fear. Like all Venezuelan girls she had been very strictly reared, very carefully sheltered from any sexual knowledge at all. In her mind now were all the terrifying stories she had heard this last year, of the *llaneros* and the unspeakable things they did to Creole women. She didn't know what those things were, but she knew her brother Fernando had said he would kill her before he let her fall into the hands of the *llaneros.*

And now here was Nicholas, terrifyingly large, alone with her in her bedroom. He was her husband, she told herself sternly, staring at him with huge, black eyes. She must do what he wished.

For the first time Nicholas was really looking at Margarita as a woman, not as a potential rival. Her hair was loose and hung over her shoulders in a shining, silken fall. It was warm brown, Beauchamp hair, the same color as his own, he noticed with a little surprise. She was sitting up against the pillows, her dark eyes fixed steadily on him, her face carefully guarded and very still. She wore a long-sleeved nightgown that was buttoned up to her chin.

He came across the floor and sat down on the edge of the bed. Amusement gleamed in the gray-green of his eyes. "You won't need that, sweetheart," he said and reached out to unbutton her gown. She said breathlessly, "I'll do it," and continued the task with hands that were not quite steady. When she had finished, she looked up at him. He raised his brows a little, and without speaking, she pulled the gown over her head.

Nicholas's eyes widened as he regarded the delicate beauty of his wife. He reached out almost tentatively to touch the small, fragile bones at the base of her throat, then moved his hand slowly down her shoulder to her breast. Her skin was like silk. He felt her shiver and looked into her eyes and said, "I don't want to hurt you, Margarita, but if this is the first time for you, it is bound to be a little painful. Is it?" Mutely she nodded in reply, and he slipped off his dressing gown and got into bed beside her. "Relax, sweetheart," he said. "It won't be so bad, really."

But Margarita could not relax. It took all her determination to force herself to remain passive in his arms, not to push him away. And, finally, when she realized what it was he wanted of her, to maintain a proud and desperate silence.

CHAPTER FIVE

Yes, it is lonely for her in her hall.
Matthew Arnold

Lady Moreton left the next day for her own home in Sussex. She had gleaned nothing from Margarita's face about how the wedding night had been and since she knew Nicholas's reputation with women, she assumed it had gone all right.

"God knows there's enough here at Winslow to keep you occupied for a while," Lady Moreton said briskly as she prepared to depart. "Nothing has been done to the house for at least forty years. It needs painting and new draperies and upholstery. Don't let Nicholas spend all the money on the property, my dear. I've spoken to Mrs. Gage, and she will be happy to take you around the house whenever you desire."

"Thank you, my lady. I hope you will have a safe journey home."

"I hope so, too, my dear." Lady Moreton hesitated, looked at the delicate, straight-browed faunlike face in front of her, then said, "Remember, my dear, you always have a friend in me."

Margarita's face broke for a moment into its rare smile. "You have been so good to me. Thank you."

She watched in silence as Lady Moreton was assisted into the waiting carriage, then turned and went back into the house. Mrs. Gage, the housekeeper, was waiting for her. "I shall be happy to show you over the house any time, my lady," the broad, ruddy-faced woman said cheerfully.

Margarita had no intention of taking Lady Moreton's advice. She knew very well how to run a large country house; her father had owned two of them as well as a plantation at San Pedro. But she thought she also knew how her attempts to take up the reins at Winslow would be regarded by Nicholas. She was an outsider, an intruder, foisted upon him against his will. Nor had she any sense of the "coming home" her grandfather had predicted. "Home" was a lovely, warm, colorful country thousands of miles away from England. She would stay here because she had to stay somewhere, but she was an alien and she knew it. She had resolved last night, after Nicholas left her, that she would keep as much out of his way as possible. Perhaps, after a while, he would simply leave her alone.

She looked now at the housekeeper's expectant face and realized she would at least have to let herself be shown over the house. They started immediately, and almost despite herself, Margarita found herself interested in Mrs. Gage's narrative. Winslow was so *old*. The two main wings of the house dated from the Jacobean era, but the architect had built them to connect the Great Hall to the two formidable towers, all of which dated from the reign of Edward III in the fourteenth century.

"The Great Hall was the main living part of the castle," Mrs. Gage explained to this stranger from South America. "During the Middle Ages the household would gather here to talk and to work and to eat." Margarita looked with interest around the enormous oak-ceilinged room. "The staircase was originally stone, but when Lord Thomas Beauchamp had the house rebuilt in the seventeenth century, he replaced the staircase with the painted wooden one you see today. It is supposedly one of the finest Jacobean staircases in the country."

"It is very lovely," Margarita murmured obediently.

Upstairs was a room that was originally Edward Beauchamp's great chamber, his personal bedroom. It had been converted into a state drawing room by the Jacobean builder, and Margarita privately thought that it looked as if no one had touched it since.

The North Wing of the house contained the state rooms and ended with the Donnington Tower, a fortification built by Edward Beauchamp, who had been, so Mrs. Gage informed Margarita, one of Edward III's most distinguished generals. Margarita was most impressed by the long gallery on the first floor. It was a beautifully paneled room whose walls were hung with portraits of the Beauchamp family. The furniture was all arranged along the walls. "The purpose of the gallery was to allow space for walking up and down on a cold or wet day," Mrs. Gage informed Margarita. Margarita thought that the gallery most probably got a great deal of use, as it seemed to her to always be cold or wet, or both, in England.

The North Wing also contained a black and white marble-floored room that was used as a dining room, a large, formal drawing room, and a "royal suite" that was intended to accommodate visiting royalty. All of the rooms had magnificent carved oak chimney pieces and molded wood ceilings, but the furnishings did look rather threadbare.

The South Wing was the area of the house Margarita was familiar with. It stretched from the Great Hall to the Lores Tower, which had been built by Edward Beauchamp's son, Guy. The rooms in this wing were smaller and more intimate, planned as a series of small suites with each room carefully proportioned to the next. Here were the family bedrooms, several sitting rooms, a smaller dining room, and the library. Now that she was looking more closely, Margarita noticed for the first time that much of the draperies and the fabrics on chairs were faded and the furniture arrangement was not particularly comfortable.

When the tour was over she smiled, graciously thanked Mrs. Gage, and told that lady to carry on exactly as she had been doing. "I will be making no changes," she said firmly, ignoring the housekeeper's startled face. And she kept her promise.

* * *

As the weeks went by, she established a routine that comforted her with a sense of familiarity. She took over the small sitting room that adjoined her bedroom and made a shelter and refuge. She had her books there, books she had gotten in London in the weeks she stayed with her grandfather. She had her needlework. She had given instructions that the fire was always to be kept going, and she would sit close to it during the long winter afternoons, her thin southern blood warmed by its glow.

She rode once a day, at eleven o'clock. It was warmer then, and she ran little chance of encountering Nicholas, who was usually in the saddle much earlier. In fact, she arranged things so that she rarely saw him until dinner time when, formally attired, she would meet him in the small paneled saloon and go in with him to the family dining room. Nicholas was usually out on the estate all day, and he radiated the vitality, the joy, the satisfaction, of someone who is doing what he most enjoys. She would listen with every appearance of interest to his enthusiastic talk of seed drills and drainage and crop rotation, and when he asked her in return what she had been doing, she always answered serenely that she had been busy with her needlework. Occasionally she had a visitor, and she would sit politely in the drawing room exchanging small talk about the weather.

It surprised her that neighboring women should call upon her. At home, women never made such calls, and she hesitantly asked Nicholas if she was expected to return them. When he replied in the affirmative, she punctiliously made the rounds of her neighbors, sitting for half an hour over a cup of tea and leaving to go home with relief to her sitting room. It was less lonely when she was alone.

* * *

The weeks went by. Nicholas was endlessly occupied by the estate during the day and was barely conscious of Margarita. Her delicate beauty drew him at night, but she never gave him any response, lying passive and quiet in his arms. She puzzled him. He sensed a reserve in her as deep as his own, and he did not know how to pierce it. His relationships with women had always been purely physical, and as such, they had been notoriously successful. He was not successful with his wife, and he did not understand why.

* * *

He was in the estate office one cold January afternoon when the door opened and Lord James Tyrrell came in. Lord James was a cousin of Sir Henry Hopkins and had been for years one of Nicholas's closest friends. They had been at school together. When he saw who it was, Nicholas rose immediately to his feet, his hand held out.

"James! What are you doing in Worcester this time of year?"

"I had to rusticate for a while—got badly dipped at Watier's last week. So I thought I'd pay a visit to old Henry and look in on you at the same time."

Nicholas's eyes surveyed his friend with cool amusement. "Cards again, eh?"

"Yes, damn it. I have no luck—unlike you, my friend. Congratulations on getting the old man's collection. It must be worth a fortune."

"I certainly hope so. Sheridan is winding up the legal details, and then I'll be free to put some of those blasted pictures on the market. They should fetch a tidy sum."

"All of which you will put into this moldering great house of yours."

"It isn't the house I'm anxious to improve, James, but the land." Nicholas spoke with a burning intensity. "Winslow could be one of the gardens of England if given the proper attention. There have been enormous advances in agriculture during the last twenty years or so. But my uncle would never put anything into the estate. The farms are run-down and unproductive, equipment is ancient and broken, and the stock is disgracefully depleted." Nicholas had acted as agent for Winslow ever since he had been sent down from school five years ago. He was painfully aware of the truth of his own words. "Winslow needs money," he concluded fiercely, "and, by God, it is finally going to get it."

Lord James looked curiously at the man seated behind the huge old desk. In many ways Nicholas was an enigma to him. If he wanted, Nicholas could be one of the major figures of London society. He was indecently good-looking, had been heir to one of the most ancient of England's titles, and had a streak of wildness in him that made him devastatingly attractive to women. But he spent only a small part of his time in London. The rest of the year he passed here at Winslow, passionately fighting a losing battle against decay. Lord James, who spent as little time as possible on his own family acres, did not understand him.

But no one could be better company when he was in the mood than Nicholas. Lord James bethought himself of some of the times they had had together and suddenly grinned. "Eleanor Rushton is not happy with your nuptials, Nick. She expressed herself quite forcibly to me on the subject."

Nicholas did not look at all perturbed. "Did she?" he said coolly.

"And she is not the only fair lady to be disappointed, although the others have not so far confided their grief to my sympathetic ear."

Nicholas grinned. "Were you very consoling, James?"

"Very." Lord James shrugged. "I wouldn't mind cutting you out with Lady Eleanor, Nick. She is a very luscious morsel. But, alas, she allowed me to hold her hand and no more."

"Keep trying," Nicholas said cynically. "She'll come around."

"Then you wouldn't mind giving her up?"

Nicholas looked amused. "Let us say, rather, that I don't mind sharing."

"Very decent of you." There was a pause, then Lord James said cautiously, "It was a bit of a shock, you know, finding out you'd been riveted."

"Yes, it came as a bit of a shock to me as well," Nicholas replied dryly. "You see, I only got the collection if I took Margarita as well."

"Good God!"

"Quite. However, it might have been worse. I might not have gotten the collection at all."

"True," said Lord James. He eyed his friend for a minute uncertainly and Nicholas laughed.

"Would you like to come up to the house with me, James, and be introduced?"

Lord James rose with alacrity. "I thought you'd never ask." Together and in perfect amity, the two young men moved toward the office door.

CHAPTER SIX

Everyone says that husbands love their wives,
  Guard them and guide them, give them happiness.
                                        Robert Browning

Nicholas settled Lord James in the drawing room with a glass of Madeira and said, "I'll go get Margarita." His butler had told him she was in her sitting room, and he had said he would go up to her himself. He wanted to explain to her first who Lord James was.

He tapped briskly on the door of the sitting room, and at her response he entered. She was seated close to the fire, a piece of needlework in her hands. He had the impression, however, that she had not been sewing but sitting idle, staring into the flames. Her eyes widened a little when she saw who it was. "My lord! Were you looking for me?"

He came into the room, and it seemed to her as if the outdoors had invaded her snug retreat. He radiated life and energy and health. "A friend of mine,

Lord James Tyrrell, has come to call and I'd like you to meet him. He is a cousin of Sir Henry Hopkins, and we've known each other since we were at Eton together."

Margarita rose instantly, anxious to remove him from her sanctuary. His very presence threatened its secure remoteness. "I shall be very pleased to meet Lord James." She put her needlework down and smoothed the soft black silk of her skirt.

He was looking curiously around the room. Books were piled on a table by the window, and a heavy black shawl lay across the back of one of the chairs. The fire was roaring. "Isn't it too warm for you, sitting so close to the fire," he asked.

"It is never too warm for me, my lord," she replied a little ruefully.

"I hadn't realized. I suppose you are accustomed to a hotter climate."

"Much hotter," said Margarita firmly. She came across the room, and he stood aside to let her precede him out the door. As he followed her downstairs, his gaze rested thoughtfully on her small, proud head and martially erect back.

She made a very deep impression on Lord James. He took one look at her grave young face and fell instantly in love. He exerted himself to the utmost to please her and entertain her and was rewarded at last with a low, rippling laugh and a totally enchanting smile. When Margarita smiled, the sun came out and Nicholas, staring in astonishment at his wife, realized for the first time that she had dimples.

Lord James finally tore himself away, and when

Nicholas came back to the drawing room after seeing him to the door, the room was empty. Margarita had vanished once again upstairs.

* * *

Nicholas began to wonder what it was his wife did during the day. He had been afraid that she would push herself in where she wasn't wanted, that she would want to take over Winslow and himself, that she would be a perpetual nuisance. None of those things had happened. As far as Winslow was concerned, Margarita might not have existed. She appeared regularly for dinner every evening, and she was there if he wanted someone in his bed at night. It should have been an ideal marriage, or so he told himself in puzzled uneasiness whenever he bothered to think about it.

He was seated in the library one rainy afternoon, absorbed in writing a letter when, out of the corner of his eye, he saw the door open and his wife appear on the threshold. She stopped dead when she saw him and, quietly, began to withdraw from the room. He looked up. "You aren't disturbing me. Please come in."

"I did not think you were here," she said a trifle breathlessly. She hesitated a moment and then came in. "I was merely going to return this and get another." She held up the book in her hand and walked swiftly to the shelves on the left-hand wall.

"What were you reading?" he asked, standing now behind his desk.

"*Candide*. You have an English translation, and my English is better than my French."

"*Candide*? I did not know young ladies read Voltaire."

She was trying to put the book back on a high shelf. "In South America, my lord, we read Voltaire. Also Rousseau and Montesquieu. We made a revolution because of those writers."

Unnoticed, he had crossed the worn carpet to stand behind her. "Let me put it back for you." He took the book from her hand and raised his arm to replace it on the shelf. Startled by his sudden appearance, Margarita flinched. He saw it and turned quickly to look at her. For a brief moment he saw into her unguarded eyes, and then the familiar shutters came down.

"You startled me," she said a little defensively, her head tipped back to look at him. He was too big. His physical presence intimidated her.

Nicholas didn't know what to say. She had flinched away from him as if she thought he were going to strike her. And for one brief moment, her eyes had been those of a child in fear. He looked into her now-expressionless face, and the thought struck him that that kind of disciplined immobility was disturbingly familiar. "You are welcome to come in here any time," he said helplessly.

She nodded with dignity. "Thank you, my lord. I will leave you now to your work." She walked with measured, unhurried steps to the door. There was no suggestion of a retreat about her, but Nicholas was suddenly quite certain that she was fleeing, and fleeing from him. She had not waited to get another book. He sat down slowly behind the desk, his eyes on the door. "Dear God," he said very softly to the unresponsive air. "What have I done?"

Something very unusual had happened to Nicholas during that brief encounter with his wife in the library. He had seen her as a person. Nicholas's distrust of women was very deep. Over the years he had grown a hard protective skin over the scar of his mother's desertion, but the wound was still there. He was not a man who could do without women, but he saw them from a purely physical point of view. His love he saved for Winslow.

But he had looked into his wife's eyes and seen there the dark, lost look of a frightened child. It was a look he recognized. He sat thinking about her, and without his quite realizing it, he was thinking about her for the first time not as "the girl" or "my wife," but simply as "Margarita."

* * *

Nicholas came back to the house in the early afternoon next day and, going upstairs, knocked at Margarita's door. "I am going to visit one of the farms this afternoon," he said. "Do you care to ride with me?" As she hesitated he added, "I think you ought to meet our tenants."

"Then of course I will come. If you do not mind waiting while I put on my riding habit?"

"I don't at all mind waiting." She looked at him expectantly, but he made no move to leave. He clearly planned to wait in her sitting room, and much as she hated to have him there, she really could not ask him to go.

"I won't be long," she said briefly, went through the door to her bedroom, and closed it behind her.

Left alone, Nicholas looked soberly around the room. There was needlework lying on the fireside chair, and this time he picked it up to look at it. The fabric, stretched over a frame, showed him the picture of a beautiful, Spanish-style house surrounded by a blaze of flowers. The needlework was exquisite, the colors brilliant.

He put the fabric down and moved to the table. There were copies of Plutarch's *Lives* and Plato's *Republic* in English, *Don Quixote* in Spanish, and two volumes each of Montesquieu and Rousseau in French. There was also a Spanish pamphlet, *Manifesto de Cartagena* by Simón Bolívar. He was holding this in his hand when Margarita came back into the room, dressed in a severe black riding habit that looked splendid on her lithe young figure.

"Do you know Bolívar?" he asked slowly, putting down the book.

"He is my cousin," she replied.

He raised his brows a little. "I know very little about what happened in Venezuela," he said frankly, "but I know he was your leader."

"He *is* our leader," she returned steadily. "The majority of the Creoles may have been destroyed, but Bolívar still lives. And while he lives, the Venezuelan Revolution is not dead."

"That revolution cost you your family," he said very gently, "yet you still hold to it?"

"If I let go of it," she returned, her voice sounding hollow in her own ears, "then I will lose them forever."

He was watching her steadily. "I see," he said quietly. And, oddly enough, he did.

* * *

CHAPTER SEVEN

Pain to thread back and to renew
Past straits, and currents long steer'd through.
                  Matthew Arnold

They went down to the stables together, and the groom brought a tall gray gelding for Margarita to ride. Nicholas was mounted on his favorite bay mare, Cora. As they moved out of the stableyard and onto the wooded path that led down from the castle's hill, he observed his wife closely. She rode beautifully, lightly poised in the saddle, her hands firm on the reins. He noticed the way those small, gloved fingers gripped the reins and felt a pang of guilt. "Have you been riding Meridian all this time?"

"Yes." Her eyes were looking forward between the horse's ears.

"He has a mouth like iron."

A dimple dented her cheek. "I've noticed."

"You ride very well." There was a pause as they safely negotiated a low-hanging branch. When he spoke again, his voice was neutral. "When I go up to London, I'll stop by Tattersall's and see about getting you a proper mount."

At that she turned to look at him. "Are you going to London?"

"As soon as I hear from Sheridan that the will has been legally cleared. I want to see about selling those damn pictures."

They had come out of the woods, and as they did, the sun broke through the gray clouds. "The pictures are very beautiful," she said to him.

He turned in his saddle and looked back at the castle. It shone silver in the winter light, elegantly placed above the slow-moving Severn which reflected back the sun's glinting rays on this cold February afternoon. "So is that," he said.

She turned to look with him, but her eyes soon moved from the castle to the profile of the man beside her. There was an expression around his hard mouth that she had never seen before. "Yes," she replied slowly. "Yes, it is."

They were going to visit Whitethorn, the largest of the farms on the Winslow estate. "George Frost is the tenant," Nicholas told Margarita as they rode side by side in the winter sunlight. "There have been Frosts at Whitethorn for as long as there have been Beauchamps at Winslow. A Frost rode with a Beauchamp in nearly every war this country has fought, from the wars of King John to the Wars of the Roses and the Civil War. Now they farm."

"As you do."

"As I do." There was the flash of unmistakable

amusement in his eyes. "Do you find that a sorry comedown from my heroic ancestors?"

"No. I find it entirely admirable." She glanced at him sidelong and found that he was watching her steadily. "At home, the people who own the land care very little about its cultivation," she explained. "Most Venezuelans think it beneath them, a 'comedown' as you say, to work as you do. A Spanish-American would judge it impossible to maintain his dignity and honor his ancestors except with pen in hand, sword at belt, or breviary before his eyes."

"Yet you think differently?"

"My father thought differently."

"Did he own much land, your father?"

"He owned two cacao plantations, twelve houses in Caracas and La Guaira, two country estates, a plantation at San Pedro, an indigo ranch, and three cattle ranches. He also owned a copper mine."

He pulled up his horse for a minute and her gray followed suit. They stood together in the lane, and he looked at her, his eyes narrowed against the afternoon sun. "And he risked it all?" he asked slowly.

"Yes. And lost it, along with his life." She nudged the gelding with her heel, and obediently he started forward again. After a moment Nicholas followed.

They did not speak again until they were almost at Whitethorn. "Is he married, this Mr. Frost?" she asked then.

"Yes." There was a pause and then he said, an odd note in his voice, "His wife is a superior woman, I believe. I think you'll like her."

* * *

He was right about Margarita's liking Emma
Frost. The two men soon disappeared to look at a
drainage ditch, and Margarita was left alone in the
cozy farm kitchen with the friendly, surprisingly
well-spoken farmer's wife. Mrs. Frost was a lawyer's
daughter who had married beneath herself, according to her family. In fact she had been perfectly
happy for thirty years married to her soft-spoken,
slow-moving George, to whom she had born six children. The youngest child, a girl of eleven, was in the
kitchen with her on this particular afternoon.

By the time Nicholas came back to collect Margarita, the two women were chatting away comfortably,
with young Susan looking on in solemn interest. As
Nicholas walked in through the door, the sound of a
baby crying came from upstairs. Margarita came instantly alert. "Do you have a baby in the house, Mrs.
Frost?"

"My son Ross's baby," the farmer's wife responded
comfortably. "She's been sleeping this past hour and
more."

Margarita was on her feet. "May I see her?" she
asked with unaccustomed eagerness.

"Take her ladyship upstairs, Susan, and see what
the baby wants," Mrs. Frost said deliberately after a
moment, and Susan obediently led the way out of the
room, with Margarita close behind her.

This left Nicholas alone in the kitchen with
Emma Frost, a position he had taken care not to be
in for many years. "Do you ever hear from your

mother, my lord?" she asked, immediately taking advantage of this rare opportunity.

His eyes looked as bleak as the sea on a dark, winter day. "No," he said tightly.

She ignored the warning implicit in his eyes and voice. "I have been worried about her for a long time. I saw in the paper a few years ago that her husband had died. I've wondered if she had enough money."

He looked at her through a long hard moment's silence, then said, with obvious reluctance, "I saw the notice as well. She is all right. I have been sending her money."

"But you won't see her?" She spoke softly, persuasively. "You don't know what her life was like in that castle, my lord. She only stayed as long as she did because of you."

He felt as if the air in the room had become thick and hard to breathe. His nostrils dilated and when he spoke, his voice had a note of such savage bitterness that it startled her. "This is not a subject I am prepared to discuss, Mrs. Frost."

As she hesitated, looking worriedly at his white, set face, there was the sound of feet on the stairs. The door opened and Margarita came in, holding a baby in her arms. "She's hungry, I think," she said to Mrs. Frost.

"My daughter-in-law should be here soon," the woman returned. "She'll have to wait until then."

Margarita bent her head and crooned something to the baby, who responded with a long cooing sound.

Margarita looked perfectly delighted and Nicholas said abruptly, "We have to be leaving, Margarita."

"All right." She carried the baby over to Mrs. Frost, talking to it softly all the time. As she handed it to the standing woman, it reached out its arms toward Margarita. She laughed, a clear, joyous sound, and raised a glowing face to Mrs. Frost. "I love babies," she said with the simplicity of absolute truth.

"Well, your ladyship, I hope you soon will have one of your own," replied the other woman placidly.

Margarita's large eyes became even larger and turned, involuntarily, to where Nicholas was standing. He could almost see the shock of a new idea registering in her mind. "Come along," he said, but not impatiently, and she nodded and walked to the door. Susan gave her her hat, which she fitted on over her smoothly-drawn-back hair.

"Goodbye Mrs. Frost," she said from the doorway. "Thank you for the tea."

"It was my pleasure, Lady Winslow," the older woman replied formally. "Please feel free to stop by for a cup any time you are near Whitethorn."

Margarita nodded gravely. "I will. Goodbye Susan." She went out the door with Nicholas close behind her. Mrs. Frost watched them exit, a small frown between her brows. Whatever their physical proximity, it was clear they were not together. She wondered if history was going to repeat itself in this new young bride at Winslow.

Mrs. Frost had been a bride herself when Charlotte Beauchamp had come to Winslow. Over the years the two women had gotten to know each other well, Charlotte finding in Emma a refuge from the icy disapproval of the castle. Christopher, even when he was home, had not been a good husband, and the earl and countess resented Charlotte's very existence, resented her presence when their own daughter had chosen to flee, resented her for bearing a son when they had been unable to produce an heir. When Charlotte eloped with John Hamilton, Emma Frost had been glad.

She sat now at her kitchen table, absently rocking the baby and thinking back. It had been five years since she saw John Hamilton's death announced. She felt deep surprise that it had been so long. Five years. She frowned. It was five years ago that Nicholas had gotten expelled from Oxford and come home to run Winslow. Mrs. Frost rocked slowly, wondering if there could be any connection between the two events.

* * *

Margarita was silent on the ride home. Nicholas was right when he thought that a new idea had taken seed in her mind. She had not thought about having a baby.

She knew, of course, that one did have babies when one was married, but she had not yet applied that knowledge to herself. Nicholas's possession of her had seemed only that, an act of possession which she must allow because she was his wife. She had not thought of it as having consequences beyond herself.

A baby. She sat before the fire in her sitting room and thought. Once she would have thought it nothing but bliss—to have a baby of her own. But now she was afraid. A baby would draw her back to life and she did not want to come. It was this she feared most in Nicholas, the force of life within him. Life was too painful, too full of anguish and fear. She wanted to stay in this winter world of blessed numbness, where she was free to bend her mind to abstract things, like philosophy and political theory. A baby was not abstract at all. A baby was real. She both dreaded and longed to have one.

* * *

That night she had a nightmare. It was the first time since she left South America that she remembered having one. All the pain and terror and loss that she had been so successfully repressing broke through into her sleep, and she was once again searching for Fernando among the dead at Aragua de Barcelona. The *llaneros* were coming closer, and she could hear the hoofbeats of their horses, but she had to find Fernando. At last she did, and looking up from his blood-streaked dead face, she saw a half-naked man grinning down at her. He reached for her and she screamed. And screamed, again and again.

Nicholas was standing in front of the fire in his bedroom taking off his shirt when he heard Margarita's scream. The sound was high and sharp with pure terror, and he flung his neckcloth aside and leaped for the door that led directly from his bedroom into hers.

She was sitting up in bed when he crashed into the room. She had stopped screaming, but he could hear the harshness of her breathing. Her hands were pressed to her mouth as if she were trying to stop the sounds by force. There was no one else in the room. He crossed the floor more quietly until he stood next to the bed. "Margarita! What happened? Are you all right?"

She stared at him for a moment with enormous fear-dilated eyes in which there was no recognition. What happened next was pure instinct on Margarita's part. She heard the deep, male voice, heard the concern in it, and threw herself into his arms, clutching him hysterically as she was swept by convulsive shuddering.

He sat down on the bed, holding her close. "Sh, now. It's all over. Everything is all right. You had a nightmare." His lips were against her hair.

After a long moment, she raised her head and her eyes flickered with recognition as she saw who it was who held her. "My lord," she whispered.

"Yes. It's me. What happened, Margarita? You frightened the life out of me, screaming like that."

"A dream. A terrible dream. The *llaneros* . . ." She broke off. "I cannot find the English."

"Never mind." He raised a gentle hand to smooth back her hair from her brow. "It is all right now."

"Yes," she whispered, her eyes clinging to his face. She was still shivering violently.

He kicked his shoes off and swung himself into

bed next to her. "Lie down here next to me," he ordered. "You're freezing."

Obediently she lay back down and very tentatively rested her head against his shoulder. Under her cheek his heartbeat was calm and unhurried and steady. He held her close. "Go back to sleep, sweetheart," he said softly. "It's all over with. You are perfectly safe now."

Slowly, very slowly, the convulsive shuddering stopped and her eyes begin to close. Nicholas was so warm. At last she relaxed into the reassuring calm and strength of his body and slept.

CHAPTER EIGHT

But a sea rolls between us—
Our different past!
Matthew Arnold

Nicholas heard four days later from Mr. Sheridan that everything was set for the sale of the paintings. "I'll be leaving for London in the morning," he told Margarita after dinner that evening. "Is there any errand I can do for you while I'm there?"

They were in the drawing room, both standing before the fire. She raised her face to him. "Yes," she said hesitantly. "If it would not be too much trouble, would you go to see Andrés Bello for me?"

He gestured her to a sofa and sat beside her. "Who is Andrés Bello?"

"He is the Venezuelan representative in London." She gave him the address. "If there is any news from home, he will have it."

He repeated the address. "I will call on him," he

said decisively. "Is that all? Is there nothing else you need?"

"No, that is all."

"Are you quite certain? You don't want some books? Some music?" Nicholas was beginning to be concerned about the amount of time she spent alone in her room.

A light gleamed in the darkness of her eyes. "Music."

"Yes. May I get you some sheet music? Do you play the piano? I have never heard you."

"No. I play the guitar."

"Splendid. I'll get you a guitar."

She looked mischievous. "You don't know anything about guitars, my lord. Ask Andrés. He will get one for you."

Nicholas was conscious of a flash of annoyance. She called this South American fellow Andrés, yet she had never addressed him as anything but "my lord."

"I have a name, Margarita," he said, and she looked at him, soberly attentive, trying to read his mood. For once his nearness did not intimidate her.

"Nicholas," she said at last, experimentally. She spoke the word as she did all her English, pronouncing each syllable distinctly and slightly emphasizing the last.

His face flashed open into a genuine smile, one of the first she had ever had from him. He looked suddenly much younger. "Nick-o-*las*," he repeated, teasingly.

A dimple flickered in her grave young cheek. "You make fun of my accent," she said reproachfully.

"I find your accent entirely admirable," he said solemnly, again mimicking her intonation, and after a moment she laughed.

* * *

He stayed in London for three weeks. Mr. Sheridan had good news for him. "I have received a very generous offer from Lord Audley for the Dutch landscapes, my lord. I strongly suggest that you take it. I doubt if you would get as much at an auction or a public sale."

Nicholas's eyes glinted at the sum. "Audley?" he said.

"The Earl of Wymondham's son."

"Oh, yes. I remember now." Nicholas grinned. "Well, he can have the Dutch with my good will. That sum will buy all new farm equipment for Winslow as well as a great deal of much-needed livestock."

"May I suggest, my lord, that you single out the pictures you don't wish to let go? I doubt it will be necessary to sell them all."

"It seems not." Nicholas rose and held out his hand. "My thanks, Mr. Sheridan. I will be in touch with you in a few days."

* * *

As he was technically mourning for his uncle, Nicholas did not grace any social events during this particular London visit. He did, however, spend a fair amount of time with Lady Eleanor Rushton.

Lady Eleanor, tall, fair, and statuesque, had had time to recover from the shock of Nicholas's marriage. She had never intended to marry him herself, being already equipped with a satisfactorily complaisant husband of her own, but she had been afraid she was going to lose him. His three week stay in London put to flight that particular worry. They spent a very considerable amount of time in bed together.

As Nicholas and Lady Eleanor's liaison had always been unabashedly sexual, Nicholas was genuinely delighted to see her again. He had scrupulously refrained from touching Margarita since his discovery in the library at Winslow, and Catherine Alnwick of Sothington, his mistress for five years, had not been in Worcestershire for weeks as she was visiting relatives in Kent. His consequent reaction to Lady Eleanor's charms pleased that lady mightily.

Nicholas also spent some satisfactory evenings touring London's various gambling and drinking clubs with Lord James Tyrrell. The new Lord Winslow got quite smashingly drunk one night and walked off with a beautiful actress who happened to be under the protection of Lord Avesbury. It took all the exertions of Lord James, who mercifully happened to be relatively sober, to avoid a duel.

Nicholas's occasional descents upon the capital tended to follow this particular pattern. It was not a pattern unfamiliar to London eyes, which were accustomed to scenes of flamboyant gambling, heavy drinking, and undisguised promiscuity. But there was a difference in the way Nicholas did things. Unlike so many of his peers, there was no aura of decadence about Nicholas, no sense that he was trying desperately to keep boredom at bay. He was, quite simply, enjoying himself. He needed to raise a little hell now and then. He was, after all, only twenty-five years old.

The big difference was that Nicholas's sojourns in London were just that, temporary vacations from his real life, which was back at Winslow. Unlike so many of his contemporaries, Nicholas was not cut off from the mainstream of life. His wildness, his drinking, his occasionally reckless exploits with horses, were mere diversions which did not disguise the fact that he was a man with a purpose in life. It was that purpose that gave him an authority far beyond his years and singled him out in the company of his peers. He was also a man who, ultimately, was most comfortable alone. In a society of people who desperately needed others to mirror back their own esteem and superiority, Nicholas needed nobody. It made him most damnably attractive.

* * *

Two days before he left London to return to Winslow, Nicholas called on his wife's countryman. Andrés Bello, scholar, poet, author, political leader, was at this time thirty-six years of age. He had been in London since 1810, when he had come with Simón Bolívar to try to raise English support for

Venezuelan independence. After a few months, Bolívar had returned to South America, bringing with him Francisco Miranda to head up the disastrous First Republic, and Andrés Bello had remained in London to continue to represent Venezuelan interests.

He greeted Nicholas with gentle courtesy. When they were seated in the shabby but comfortable study, the South American looked at Nicholas closely, his brown eyes searching. "So you are the husband of our little Margarita," he said softly. His English was perfectly fluent, lightly accented. "I hope she is well?"

"She is well," Nicholas answered. He stared back, unsmiling, at the Spanish American. "She asked me to call on you for the latest news from Venezuela."

"Ah." Andrés Bello shifted a little in his chair. "It is not good, Lord Winslow. The only positive thing you can tell Margarita is that Boves is dead. But so, alas, is Ribas. The only remaining Republican stronghold is Margarita Island. The Royalists hold the entire mainland."

Nicholas frowned. "I know very little about the Venezuelan war, Senor Bello, and I don't like to upset my wife by asking her. Who, for instance, is Boves?"

"Who is Tomás Boves?" Andrés Bello repeated, impassive. His voice had lost its gentle note. "You are right not to ask Margarita about Tomás Boves, my lord. Among other things, he killed her father."

Nicholas made no answer, sitting quietly, waiting for the American to continue. After a moment he did, looking tired and tense, and speaking with obvious restraint. "Tomás Boves was a smuggler who led the Royalist forces against the Republic. He was a man of unparalleled brutality. He loved cruelty. One of his favorite pastimes was to skin the feet of his captives and force them to walk on broken glass."

"He was a smuggler?" Nicholas asked in a hard voice, after the other man had paused for a moment.

"Yes. He was jailed by the Republic for smuggling, and when he was released, he turned into its greatest enemy. It was he who raised the *llaneros*."

Nicholas's brows snapped together. He recognized the word. "What are the *llaneros*?" he asked.

"Men who live on the *llanos*." At Nicholas's puzzled look he went on to explain further. "The *llanos* are the plains of the Orinoco valley. They are like the pampa of the La Plata: limitless grass steppes unbroken by trees. For thousands of square miles nothing grows except tough grass, as high as a man. It is one of the greatest pastures of the world and home of Venezuela's great cattle ranches.

"The men who live in the *llanos* are tough, savage, warlike, barely human. It is a hard land to live by, baked by the sun for six months and flooded by hundreds of rain-gorged streams for the other six. Its inhabitants are jaguars, crocodiles, snakes, pumas, lethal insects, and the *llaneros*.

"Tomás Boves knew the *llanos* and knew that an army of *llaneros* was the kind of barbaric horde that would subdue Venezuela. The *llaneros* murder for pleasure and torture for pastime. Boves left a train of horror and blood wherever he went; women and children were the victims of his bloody diversions, as well as any captives he might take in battle.

"One of your wife's brothers, Ramón, was killed at La Puerta last June. In that battle Boves, with eight thousand men, caught Bolívar who had only twenty-three hundred. Half of the Republicans were left dead on the field, including Ramón, who was acting as Bolívar's secretary.

"In July, Valencia surrendered to Boves after a siege that lasted a month. They had no water and no food left. Boves promised mercy. He killed the siege's leader, who happened to be Don Antonio Carreño, Margarita's father. He then proceeded to annihilate the town.

"Boves then headed for Caracas, but all he found there were the old and the sick. Everyone else had left, fleeing with Bolívar to the coast rather than staying to face Boves's tender mercies. Margarita and her brother Fernando were among the Caraqueños who went with Bolívar. In August, Fernando, the last living member of your wife's family, was killed at the Battle of Aragua de Barcelona.

"Margarita was one of the few to make it to the Cumaña, where, thank God, your uncle's English captain found her and took her off. On October 16, Boves occupied Cumaña and cut the throats of everyone in the town, women and children included."

"Jesus Christ," said Nicholas. In the harsh light from the window, his face was as hard as stone. "I had no idea of any of this."

"Venezuela is a small country, many thousands of miles away," Andrés Bello said wearily. "You English have just concluded a war of your own. It is understandable that you do not know about what happened to us."

"So it is over?" Nicholas asked carefully.

Andrés Bello's face looked very stern. "It is not over. Nearly one third of our citizens may be dead, but one man is still alive. Tell Margarita that Boves is dead and Bolívar lives. He is in Cartagena and he will come again."

"Bolívar," said Nicholas slowly. "Margarita said the same thing, that while Bolívar lives the Venezuelan Revolution is not dead."

Andrés Bello's face relaxed into a smile. "She is, after all, the daughter of Don Antonio Carreño. The revolution was plotted in the rooms of her house by her father and her brothers, among others. And Margarita herself was instrumental in the expulsion of the captain-general in April 1810."

Nicholas's eyes were narrowed. "In 1810," he said, "my wife was twelve years old."

"I know." Andrés Bello's smile softened even further. "The loveliest child in all South America, she was, the little Margarita. Half the young men in Caracas were simply waiting for her to grow up."

"What happened in 1810?" Nicholas asked patiently.

Andrés Bello leaned a little forward. "There were a group of us gathered in the Carreño house in Caracas; many of the members of the Caracas Cabildo—the town council, you would say—were there. The royal family had been deposed in Spain, you understand, and we were deciding what we should do: denounce Napoleon and declare our allegiance to the Spanish monarchy, or declare our independence.

"In the middle of the discussion the door opened and Margarita came in, carrying a pitcher of cold juice. I remember how Don Antonio put his arm about her waist and said, half-jokingly, 'And you, little one, do you feel allegiance to the King of Spain?'

"She looked back at him very gravely. 'Why should I feel allegiance to the King of Spain, Papa?' she answered. 'I am not Spanish. I am American.'"

Andrés Bello leaned back and half closed his eyes. "I remember how we all sat there, silent, looking at that beautiful child. That afternoon—it was Holy Thursday—the Cabildo met with the captain-general. The result of that meeting was that he was escorted down to La Guaira and put aboard a Spanish man-of-war." He opened his eyes and looked directly at Nicholas. "And that is how, Lord Winslow, the first independent government in South America came into being."

Nicholas smiled a little. "'And a little child shall lead them,'" he quoted.

Andrés Bello looked pleased. "Precisely, my lord."

"I am glad you told me all this," Nicholas said. "It helps to explain a great deal about Margarita."

"She has had a very terrible time of it, the little one," Andrés Bello said. "And she had been so sheltered. Her father and her brothers would not allow the wind to blow too harshly on Margarita. You must try to be kind to her."

"Yes," Nicholas said briefly and got to his feet. "Oh, there is one more thing, Senor Bello. I promised her I would bring her back a guitar. Perhaps you might help me in this matter?"

"Certainly, Lord Winslow. I should be most happy to purchase one for you and have it sent to your house."

They stood together in the doorway for a moment, Nicholas towering over the slender Spanish American. "If you should care to visit us at Winslow sometime," he said, "we should be happy to see you."

"Thank you, Lord Winslow," Andrés Bello responded gently. "You are very kind."

CHAPTER NINE

For I that danced her on my knee,
   That watch'd her on her nurse's arm,
   That shielded all her life from harm,
At last must part with her to thee.
                   Tennyson

It was a thoughtful Nicholas who drove home to Winslow a few days later. An image of his wife's young and guarded face was before his eyes, and the words of Andrés Bello were in his ears. "She has had a very terrible time of it, the little one," he had said. "You must try to be kind to her." Nicholas, rather surprisingly, had every intention of trying to be.

It was late afternoon by the time he reached Winslow. He found his wife in her sitting room. She rose when he came in and said softly, "Welcome home, my lord."

He stood in the shadow of the doorway looking at her. "Did you get my letter saying when to expect me?"

"Yes. Thank you for writing."

Her face looked very pale in the firelight, and

there were shadows under her eyes. "Are you all right?" he asked abruptly.

"I am fine." He came across to stand next to her and tipped her face up. She stood quite unresisting, looking up at him, waiting for what he would do next.

"You look tired," he said.

"Perhaps I am, a little."

He let go of her chin. "Come into your bedroom and see what I've brought you."

Her dark eyes sparkled a little. "A guitar?"

"Come and see," he repeated and stood aside for her to precede him.

Lying on her bed was a guitar. Next to it was a wine-velvet cloak. "Oh," said Margarita softly. "For me?" At his nod she went over to the bed and picked it up. It was floor-length and fully lined with sable.

"Nicholas," she breathed.

That should help to keep you warm in this cold English climate."

She came to him then and touched him lightly on the arm. He thought that she could not have ventured to touch a complete stranger more tentatively. "Thank you," she said, and her grave face flashed for a moment its rare smile.

"You are most welcome," he replied. "After dinner I expect a sample of that guitar."

* * *

He had to postpone his guitar concert. Margarita was paler than ever at dinner, and although she made a pretense of eating, in actuality she consumed almost nothing. It was not until dinner was almost over that he noticed these things, having been occupied in giving her a strictly edited version of his visit to London. When dinner was over, he sent her to bed. "You look exhausted," he said to her in the drawing room. "You can try the guitar tomorrow. Go to bed and get some sleep." His voice had a note of protective authority she recognized, and automatically, she obeyed.

After breakfast the following morning, he came back upstairs and tapped at her door. He wanted to take her to the stables to see the filly he had bought for her to ride. There was no answer, and he was raising his arm to rap more sharply when there came to his ears the unmistakable sounds of someone being sick. He opened the door and walked in. Margarita was bent over the basin on her nightstand, retching uncontrollably. He strode across the room and put an arm around her, supporting her against him. When the attack was over, he wiped her face with his handkerchief and lifted her back into bed.

When she was reclining against the pillows, he searched her face. It was pinched and sallow looking. Her eyes told him nothing, wide and dark and fathomless. "How long have you been ill like this?" he asked sharply. "I am going to send for the doctor."

"There is nothing wrong. He has already come. I am going to have a baby, that is all."

His eyes flickered with surprise. "A baby?"

"Yes."

His finely cut nostrils were a little dilated. "When?"

"In October, I believe."

"I see." He looked at her in some concern. "Are you sick like that all the time?"

"It is worst in the morning. The doctor says that after three months it usually passes."

"Three months!" He sat down on the side of the bed and picked up her hand. He stared for a moment at her wrist, exposed by the sleeve of her night dress. It looked so frail, so delicately veined and fragile against his own big hand. "A baby," he said slowly. "I can't quite take it in."

She gazed at him for a moment longer with that unreadable face, and then she suddenly smiled at him. It was a smile he had never seen before and in her eyes were acknowledgment and recognition. "I know," she said softly.

His hair had fallen over his forehead, like a schoolboy's, and the line of his mouth as he looked at her was unexpectedly tender. "You stay in bed," he said, and he did not mean it as a suggestion. "I'll get someone to clean this up." He rose from the bed. "Did you have Dr. Macrae?"

"Yes."

"I'll speak to him."

"Yes."

"Try to get some sleep."

"I will try," she said obediently and closed her eyes. He stood looking for a minute at the dark lashes as they lay on her pale cheek. Quietly, he left the room.

* * *

She insisted on dressing and coming down to dinner. He had protested when she first appeared, but she would not allow herself to be sent back upstairs. "I wish to join you at dinner," she said stubbornly and he had acquiesced. It was as though she had set herself a standard of behavior and clung to it fiercely.

He watched her all through dinner. Everything about her was so delicately made: the straight, slender brows, the fastidious nose, the curves of her mouth. Yet her back, straight as a lance, never once touched the back of her chair. There was steel in that back, and endurance and strength. This small, slender girl had already in her short life shown a power of resistance and of survival far beyond what he had ever had to demonstrate.

After dinner he told her what Andrés Bello had said. "I am glad Boves is dead," she said after a minute. "I would very much have liked to kill him myself." The lines of her mouth were severe. She meant it.

"I heard something further," he went on slowly. "Not from Senor Bello, from someone in the government. Spain is sending a great expedition against South America. It is to be commanded by General Morillo: five warships, over forty transports, and ten thousand soldiers was my information. One of the most imposing expeditions ever to leave a Spanish port. It may have sailed already."

"Madre de Dios," said Margarita.

"Spain does not want to lose its empire."

"It will, though." There was a little frown of concentration between her brows. "In fact, this sending of a fleet may prove to be a very good thing."

"How so?"

"The war so far has been a war carried on by the Criollos, the upper class," she said seriously. "The rest of Venezuela, the pardos, the Indians, the *llaneros*, they either did not care or they fought, not *for* Spain but *against* us. They had no concept of national liberty."

Her lovely face was very somber. "Let them taste the tender mercies of Spanish rule, and independence will seem sweet. Bolívar will come back and the final war will commence, a war of Venezuelans against Spaniards, a war of independence."

He was listening to her intently, his greenish eyes narrowed in concentration. "There is one thing in all this I do not understand. You tell me it was the aristocrats who made the revolution. You told me of all your father's possessions; he was obviously a very wealthy man, a very influential man. Why would such a man, such a class of men, wish to change the established order?"

Those grave, level eyes of hers were steady on his face. "You find it strange to contemplate the spectacle of a revolution planned and carried out by those who had everything to lose by it."

"Precisely."

"George Washington was one of the richest men in all North America," she pointed out.

"Yes, I suppose he was." He grimaced a little. "You must think me most damnably materialistic."

"No. I think you have never known what it is to feel that foreigners are running your country when you are perfectly capable of running it yourself. How would you like it, my lord, if the only people who could sit in the English Parliament were Spaniards—Spaniards, born in Spain, I mean. No one born in England would be eligible."

There was the sound of a log falling on the fire. "I see what you mean," he said.

"I thought perhaps you might."

* * *

The sickness did not get better, and Margarita was forced to go to bed and stay there. At first she could not lift her head from the pillow without being sick; it took all her concentration and energy to keep down a few spoonfuls of broth. Gradually the sickness got better, and she was able to sit up a little and even to read a bit.

Nicholas was worried about her and, during the two months she was in bed, would come faithfully every night after dinner to sit with her, to talk with her, to read to her. He had searched his library without success for a novel that would appeal to her and would have no mention of war. Upon his mentioning his dilemma to Catherine Alnwick, she had given him a copy of *Pride and Prejudice*, which he read with an enjoyment he had not expected. He and Margarita laughed over Mr. Collins and Lady

Catherine de Bourgh, sympathized with Jane and Elizabeth and went from despising to admiring Mr. Darcy. After they finished *Pride and Prejudice*, he borrowed *Mansfield Park*, and they enjoyed that as well.

Margarita's attitude toward Nicholas had altered after the night she woke up screaming in terror and he had comforted her. It changed even more during the months she lay in bed. Far from dreading his presence, she found herself looking forward to his visits. Health and strength and steadiness walked into the room when Nicholas came; he made her feel she *would* get well, would be able to once again do the things she wanted. As she lay listening to his strong, even, clear voice reading Jane Austen to her, she felt more at peace than she had in over a year.

CHAPTER TEN

> ... and in my breast
> Spring wakens too, and my regret
> Becomes an April violet.
>   Tennyson

It was a lovely spring morning in April when Nicholas took Margarita out into the garden for the first time. She drew in her breath in wonder and delight at the sight of the daffodils, whose golden heads greeted her first excursion out-of-doors since February. The world had awakened. The sun was warm on their heads, the scent of the damp earth was in their nostrils.

"I always think the advantage of living in a climate like this is that you have spring," said Nicholas. "In a country like Venezuela, where one is constantly surrounded by flowers, how can one feel the sense of wonder, of *deliverance*, that the first daffodils of spring have here? The deadness of winter is over. The earth is alive again. It is like a resurrection."

She listened to him and then bent to cup her

hands around one of the brilliant yellow flowers. It felt so cool and delicate under her fingers. She stared at its sunny beauty and knew that Nicholas was right. She felt herself coming back as well, from the shadows into the light. But I can't *bear* it, she thought. She released the flower and stood up. "They are very beautiful," she said in a low voice.

Her face had the dark, lost look he had seen on it only a few times before. "Don't you want this child, Margarita?" he asked gently. "I thought, from what you said to Mrs. Frost, that you would be happy."

"It is hard to be happy when you are sick."

"I know. But I thought you were better."

"I am. It is—oh, it is so difficult to explain what I feel."

"Try." He guided her to a stone bench and they sat down.

"It is that I feel I have no right to be happy, no right to be sitting here in this lovely sunshine. There is too much suffering, there has been too much suffering, for me to be happy."

"I see." He spoke slowly, carefully, seeking to find the right words. "It is *not* wrong of you to be happy if you can be. It would be wrong of you to deny in yourself all those feelings and hopes and dreams your people fought for. You owe it to them to live the fullest life you possibly can, to use all the talents your parents so carefully nurtured in you. Do you think your father would be proud of you for being unhappy?"

Her profile was pure and delicate and unresponsive. "No," she said. He looked from her to the daffodils, and when he looked back her head was bent. He saw a tear fall onto her wrist, and he reached out to put an arm around her. He could feel her holding herself hard, trying not to let the tears come. He put his cheek against her hair.

"I am so sorry, little one," he said softly. "I have been so unkind to you."

At that she turned into his arms. Everything inside her was broken and bleeding, and she wept as she had never wept before. She was exhausted when it was all over, and he carried her back into the house and upstairs to her bed.

* * *

It was a beautiful spring. Margarita walked in the garden and rode around the estate, sometimes with Nicholas and sometimes alone. The apple orchards were magnificent, with enormous blooms that kindled the unaccustomed joy within her. The scent of lilacs hung in the air and the soft breeze ruffled her hair when she took off her hat. She was conscious, too, of the child within her. The sense of life, of creation, was very strong in her now. She was profoundly aware of this new life she was carrying, she was creating. She had wanted so desperately to do something to counter the destruction she had seen all around her in Venezuela. And now she felt she was. She was creating a life. She was putting something back into the emptied world.

The scars of the revolution were still there. They showed in the recurring nightmares that troubled her sleep. They showed, too, in her hypersensitivity to pain or death. The sight of a wounded animal upset her dreadfully. She could not even bear to kill the spider who had made a web in the corner of her sitting room.

But once again she belonged to life. It was Nicholas who had done this for her, and she looked to him with gratitude and thankfulness. He was her rock, her fortress, her bulwark. She thanked God on her knees every night that he had given her Nicholas.

* * *

Nicholas was both moved and frightened by the change in Margarita. The depths of her feelings, the intensity of her response to even the ordinary things of life, awed him a little. She was too vulnerable. It was not safe to be that vulnerable. He felt responsible for her and sometimes, when he looked at her, he felt the responsibility was too great.

She asked nothing of him. Of all people, Margarita was one of the last who would ever intrude where she felt she was not wanted. She never once tried to broach the solitariness that was at the core of him. She was content with his presence when he chose to bestow it upon her, and she became increasingly interested in the work he was doing on the estate. Because she never pressed him, he shared more with her than he had with any other person since his mother. He felt a closeness to her that was human rather than sexual.

He had not approached her for sex since he had

come back from London. At first she had been too sick, and then, as she began to get better, he too was conscious of the child. He was afraid, as well, afraid to shatter the happiness he could see growing in her along with the baby. She never once made a gesture that would indicate that she would welcome the resumption of any kind of physical relationship with him. She seemed, he thought somewhat ruefully, to regard him as a surrogate big brother.

It was a situation he did not find totally satisfactory, but he accepted it. And went regularly, several afternoons a week, to visit Catherine Alnwick at Sothington.

Catherine Alnwick was thirty-six years of age and a widow. She had two boys, both of whom were at Eton. She went to London for a few months each spring, but most of the time she lived in Worcestershire. Her relationship with Nicholas had been going on since he came home to Winslow five years ago. The death of her husband four years ago had only made things easier and less risky for them.

Catherine was a very beautiful, very independent woman. She had only been thirty-two when her husband died, but she showed no signs of interest in marrying again—and she had had a number of chances. When she went to London she moved in the best of circles; she had friends and relatives who owned country homes all over England and she was invited to visit regularly; she had plenty of money. But she remained a widow. Her sisters did not understand it, but then her sisters knew nothing of Nicholas.

Catherine was very satisfied with their relationship. She had no great desire to marry again; the freedom of widowhood suited her very well. She did what it pleased her to do and had to account to no one. Nicholas was the perfect solution for her. He aroused her more than any man she had ever known. Even after five years, the sight of him riding up her driveway was enough to start her pulses pounding. He satisfied her body and made no claims on her freedom. She went to London when she liked, visited whom she liked, slept with whom she liked. And he did the same. Obviously he had found their relationship as satisfactory as she; he had held to her for over five long years, and his marriage did not seem to be posing any obstacles at all.

Catherine had never met Margarita. She had not been in Worcestershire last winter when the local gentry were paying calls on the new bride at Winslow, and she was intensely curious, to meet her. "Really, my dear," she said to him humorously, as he was leaving one afternoon, "you are turning into a recluse. Jane Hopkins was asking me only yesterday if I thought you would be offended by an invitation to dine at Twinings."

"Offended?" His strongly marked brows drew together. "Why on earth should I be offended?"

"No one in the neighborhood has seen you since last winter. People are not quite sure how to regard you. You have been rather brutally refusing invitations, you know."

"My wife has been sick."

"I realize that. But she is better now, you say. I

think it is time you made your reentry into the neighborhood, Nicholas."

He looked down at her, a faintly sardonic smile on his lips. "Do you Cat? All right. Tell Lady Hopkins to send her invitation."

She felt, uncomfortably, that he was reading her too accurately, but she replied calmly enough, "I will."

Two days later the invitation arrived at Winslow and was duly answered in the affirmative.

CHAPTER ELEVEN

Smoake can never burne, they say,
But the flames that follow may.
Thomas Campion

Margarita was a little nervous about making her first appearance in English society, but she comforted herself with the thought that Nicholas would be beside her. She had met three of the people who would be at Twinings before, but she had no clear recollection of them. She had been so frozen with unhappiness last winter that nothing and no one had registered very clearly on her consciousness.

She had a new dress to wear. Nicholas had insisted that she give up her eternal black, and so this last month a dressmaker from the village had made her some new clothes. "After the baby, I will take you to London for a completely new wardrobe," he told her. "I suppose it wouldn't make much sense to do it now."

Her dimples appeared. "What I need at the moment, my lord, are dresses that can be let out easily. Most decidedly, a new wardrobe should wait until after the baby is born."

Margarita was actually looking very well. The high-waisted styles were an advantage, and although if you looked at her closely her pregnancy showed, the dress concealed it to a large degree. She wore a gown of delicate rose-pink silk, scooped low in the front. It had small puffed sleeves and the skirt that fell from its high waistband was a little fuller than style dictated. Her hair was knotted smoothly on top of her head, and in her ears and around her throat hung the famous Winslow diamonds.

Nicholas smiled with pleasure when he saw her. "You look lovely," he told her approvingly.

In return, Margarita regarded her husband. She reached up to smooth back a lock of hair that had fallen over his forehead. "Were you writing in the library?" she asked severely.

He grinned. "Guilty."

"I can always tell by the way you tug at your poor hair." She stepped back. "There, it looks tidy enough now." She picked up her cloak. "I am ready if you are."

"Margarita!" He stared at her cloak. "Surely you don't need that! It is June."

She handed the sable-lined cloak to him. "It is already feeling a little chilly, and by the time we come home it will be cold."

He sighed and draped it over her shoulders. "I was positively hot all afternoon."

"*You* go around half the winter without even a

coat," she replied accusingly. "Clearly you have no sensitivity to cold at all. I have."

"So I have observed."

She smiled at him. "You are teasing me, my lord, and it is very nice of you to try to take my mind off this party. You will promise not to desert me if there are cards?"

Nicholas had warned her that it was likely that Lady Hopkins would get up a few tables of whist. He had been teaching her how to play, but she was still very much a beginner. "I promise," he said.

* * *

The dinner party consisted of Sir Henry and Lady Hopkins, Lord James Tyrrell, who was visiting them again, Mrs. Alnwick, Mr. Knight, who owned Eversly Manor a few miles away, and his wife, Lady Anne, who was a daughter of the Earl of Lawnthorpe. The only ones who had ever met the new Lady Winslow were the residents of Twinings; the rest of the company were politely but definitely curious.

Catherine Alnwick found herself staring in great surprise at Margarita; somehow she had not expected her to look like this. "How do you do, Mrs. Alnwick," Nicholas's wife said in a low, clear voice. "I am pleased to make your acquaintance."

Catherine said something in reply and Margarita passed on to Lord James Tyrrell, who bowed over her hand with reverence. Catherine's eyes went from the face of his wife to Nicholas, but she could discern nothing behind the pleasant, courteous expression on his too-good-looking face.

They went into dinner. Margarita sat next to Sir Henry and on her other side was Mr. Knight. Nicholas, chatting lightly with Catherine Alnwick, saw that she was charming the two older men effortlessly. She was so modest, yet so attentive and aware, with her big brown eyes and soft gravity. Mr. Knight, who was often stiff and haughty with strangers, was smiling at her genially and telling her about his dogs, which he was famous for breeding. By the time the last course was served he had offered her a puppy. "Come and choose one for yourself, Lady Winslow. Get your husband to bring you. We'll be glad to see you any time."

Nicholas, hearing this, said to Catherine Alnwick, "Knight has just offered Margarita a puppy. If she can accomplish that in the course of one dinner, I ought to enroll her in the diplomatic corps." His voice was softly amused and she looked at him sharply.

"She is very lovely. And so young."

He slanted a look at her, eyebrows raised. "She is eighteen," he said. "You knew that."

"Yes, I suppose I did." She smiled a little ruefully. "What I meant to say was that she *looks* so young. I suppose I must be feeling old."

A flash of amusement came and went in his face. "I shouldn't worry, Cat. You are looking very lovely yourself tonight. I always like you in blue."

The rest of the company was surreptitiously watching this low-voiced exchange between Nicholas and Catherine. There wasn't a person in the room, including the servants, who didn't know about Nicholas Beauchamp and Mrs. Alnwick. They also knew that his marriage did not seem to have interrupted the most famous secret liaison in the neighborhood. They looked from Catherine and Nicholas to Margarita, who was listening to Mr. Knight. There was not a shadow on her serene young brow. Obviously, they all thought, "the wife" had not yet found out.

* * *

Margarita bore up very well under the polite but relentless scrutiny of the ladies when they retired after dinner to the drawing room. She was conversing amicably with Catherine Alnwick when the gentlemen joined them. Catherine was surprised to find she did not at all feel as if she were talking to a young girl; there was a dignity and graciousness about Margarita that was rarely seen in English girls of her age.

As Nicholas had surmised, Lady Hopkins set about arranging two tables of whist. She was about to suggest that Margarita play with Lord James when Nicholas said easily, "If you do not mind, Lady Hopkins, I will partner my wife."

"Of course I do not mind," replied Lady Hopkins, good breeding effectively concealing her surprise.

"You see," Margarita explained with a shy smile, "I am just learning to play, and my lord is so patient with me." At that Lady Hopkins did stare in surprise. Patience was not one of Nicholas's more well-known virtues.

They played against Catherine Alnwick and Lord James Tyrrell. Catherine was a very fine card player and usually partnered Nicholas, who was himself an excellent and demanding player. It soon became clear that Margarita was not in their class, although she did not do badly for a rank beginner. "I did not know you had that card," she said to Nicholas after he had played the king of hearts.

"When the king was not played earlier, you should have known Lord Winslow had it," Catherine explained kindly.

Margarita frowned a little, going over the play in her mind. She nodded. "Yes, I see." She looked at her husband. "I should have led a heart back to you, should I not?"

"Yes, but there's not much damage done. I was able to use it after all."

Margarita sighed. "There are so many things to remember. I will never learn it all."

"You are doing very well, Lady Winslow," said Lord James reassuringly. "In fact, you and Nick are winning."

"That is because Lord Winslow has drawn all the cards tonight," Catherine said a trifle tartly.

"It has been a lucky night," Nicholas agreed suavely.

Catherine shot him a look from under her lashes. There was a smile touching the corner of his mouth as he regarded his cards. She looked at that firm, well-cut mouth and then forced her eyes back to her own hand. Margarita tentatively laid a card on the table and Nicholas smiled at her warmly. "Good girl," he said and she flushed with pleasure.

Afterwards, over tea, the conversation became more general. Margarita, seated by the fire, was feeling extremely sleepy and wondered how long it would be before she disgraced herself and yawned. Nicholas, noticing her growing silence, looked at her intently. Her back was as straight as ever, her head was erect. Her eyes were black and enormous, and seemed to engulf her small face. He leaned across to ask her softly, "Are you tired?"

She looked like a child caught out in mischief. "A little."

Ten minutes later, they were seated in their carriage on the way home to Winslow. Everyone had been most understanding and Mr. Knight had patted her paternally on the shoulder. "Your husband is quite right," he said. "You must be sure to get proper rest. Mind now, don't forget the puppy."

"I won't, Mr. Knight. I should love a puppy," she responded softly.

"I am glad to see Winslow is taking care of her," Mr. Knight announced to the remaining company. "She seems a very sweet little thing."

Lady Anne and Lady Hopkins exchanged glances. They agreed that Margarita seemed a very sweet little thing. They agreed that Nicholas did indeed seem very attentive. Both ladies looked with veiled speculation to Catherine Alnwick, but her lovely face gave nothing away.

CHAPTER TWELVE

But in the world I learnt, what there
Thou too wilt surely one day prove,
That will, that energy, though rare,
Are yet far, far less rare than love.
Matthew Arnold

Margarita and Nicholas did pay a visit to Mr. Knight and went home with an adorable spaniel puppy that Margarita called Eva. The little bitch became her faithful companion, walking with her in the gardens and riding beside her in the old-fashioned phaeton that Nicholas had taught her to drive.

She loved to drive around the estate, surveying the fields of ripening wheat and oats and growing vegetables. The orchards were lovely and loaded with fruit. The cattle grazed peacefully in the summer sun. The fruitfulness of the land was a balm to her spirit. She found herself endlessly interested in Nicholas's schemes; after the destruction and death she had seen in South America, making things grow seemed to her the most wonderful of ambitions.

Nicholas expanded under her interest. He was

used to being regarded as freakish for his passionate interest in agriculture. Even in those who were outwardly sympathetic, like Catherine Alnwick, he detected a note of amused bewilderment. It was all very well to want to improve one's property, but no one thought it necessary for Nicholas to spend his days in the fields.

His devotion to the land, to Winslow land in particular, had manifested itself after his mother's elopement. He had been left rootless, without an object on which to focus his quite considerable capacity for love. People, particularly women, seemed to him untrustworthy. Never again, a ten-year-old Nicholas had sworn, never again would he let himself be hurt as his mother had hurt him.

And so his love turned to Winslow: to the land that had belonged to his family for seven hundred years, to the land that would one day belong to him. Like Margarita, he found enormous satisfaction in making things grow. He had never been able to share this satisfaction with anyone, until she came.

He worried about her driving around by herself. He had refused to let her go out alone until he was satisfied that she was competent holding the reins, and the horse he insisted she drive was placid and steady. He understood very well her dislike of having a groom with her; he too preferred to be alone. And he was delighted that she wanted to get out of the house. So he crossed his fingers and let her go, and she managed very well. Several times a week he would run into her on one of the small roads that crisscrossed the Vale, ambling along in the sun, a straw bonnet on her brown head, and Eva perched up beside her. He always turned his horse to walk beside her for a while, and her small face, upturned toward him, would glow with pleasure.

At night, after dinner, they took long walks in the summer twilight, sometimes talking, sometimes silent, absorbed in their own thoughts. As her body thickened with the child, Nicholas insisted that they confine themselves to the gardens and stay off the hill, but still they walked every evening. Then they would go in for tea, and afterwards Margarita would go upstairs to bed.

It was a time of healing for Margarita. She had begun to correspond with Andrés Bello and his letters usually left her depressed for days, but it was not the all-enveloping misery she had suffered last winter. The Spanish fleet had reached South America, and the first action of the commander, Morillo, was to take Margarita Island. The Republicans had no base left in Venezuela. Bolívar left Cartagena and was in Jamaica, trying to interest the British in aiding his cause. Andrés Bello wrote her that there was no chance the British would intervene; their relations wth Spain were too tenuous.

It was a great help to her to be able to talk to Nicholas. She felt that he alone seemed to understand what it was she was feeling. She was right in that he did understand. Nicholas knew all too well what it felt like to be left alone in the world. Margarita's family had been torn from her by violence, but she, at least, was confident of their enduring love. She was a devout Catholic and derived much comfort from the conviction that she was not eternally separated from those she loved. She had never suffered the pain of a love that was betrayed and rejected. Nicholas had, and because of that he was armored against allowing himself to become too involved with other people. Margarita, on the contrary, suffered agonies at the thought of what the Spanish were doing to her countrymen. Nicholas was apprehensive for her; it was not safe to feel so much.

He was aware that he worried about his wife. For some reason he could not articulate, he felt personally responsible for her. All the protectiveness in his nature had suddenly narrowed and focused on this one human being. He was not a man given to self-analysis, so he did not realize that this feeling stemmed from the first time he had looked into her eyes and seen there a lost and frightened child. He had recognized instantly, emotionally, that look, and from then on, he had felt it his personal mission to shield her from any further pain.

He had to go to London in early September and when he left, Margarita felt lost. She went to visit Mrs. Frost every day, something she did not usually do so frequently. Mrs. Frost was a great consolation to her. She talked sensibly about childbirth and children and dispelled many of Margarita's fears about her coming ordeal. She talked too about Nicholas's mother, whom she obviously remembered with a great deal of affection.

"My lord never mentions his mother at all," Margarita said gravely. "I thought she was dead."

Mrs. Frost looked at her own capable hands as

they sewed a hem on a shirt. "Lord Winslow loved his mother very much. I think he can't forgive her for leaving him, for preferring someone else. He was too attached to her, I suppose. When she left he had no one." She sighed. "I'm sure she loves him still. His refusal to see her must hurt bitterly."

Margarita's brown eyes looked huge. "It is very sad."

She found the information she heard from Mrs. Frost of very great interest, but she never mentioned his mother to Nicholas. Margarita had the Spanish sense of family. It was this sense that had prompted her to write to her grandfather about her mother's death three years ago. She determined that when her baby was born, she would write to Nicholas's mother.

Three days before Nicholas returned, she received a letter from Andrés Bello. In it was the information that the Spanish were besieging Cartagena. That night she opened her window and looked out at the sky. The night was clear and the stars were brilliant. She felt a kind of peace enter her as she looked up at the vast and remote heavens. What did all their little earthly sufferings and strivings matter in the face of that magnificence? She stayed at the window for a long time, reluctant to relinquish the peace she knew she felt only at the price of turning her back on life. She felt empty and free. And then the child within her kicked, and slowly she closed the window and got into bed.

Nicholas arrived shortly before dinner on September 24. It had been softly raining all day, and there were beads of moisture on his hair as he came into Margarita's bedroom where she was dressing for dinner. A rush of joy went through her at the sight of him, so big and damp and vibrant. She felt life and hope coursing back into her veins. "I am glad to see you, my lord," she said. "I missed you."

He bent to kiss her forehead. "I am glad to be back. How are you and the baby doing?"

"We are very well, thank you."

He was scanning her with narrowed eyes, checking the truth of her statement. She was big with child, but her arms, throat, and shoulders still retained their old slimness. There was the suggestion of a shadow below her eyes. "Has the weather been getting you down?" he asked lightly.

"A little. But it is like sunshine to have you home again. Did your business prosper?"

"I'll tell you about it at dinner," he said. "First I must change."

* * *

Nicholas's sojourn in London this time had been rather different from his last visit. He spent a good deal of time with his lawyer and his man of business, both of whom were delighted to see that the new Earl of Winslow showed every sign of taking his responsibilities very seriously indeed. They were surprised. Nicholas's reputation had not prepared them for this startling transformation.

In fact, most of his London acquaintances knew very little about Nicholas. He had never spent much time in London. He had never shown any interest at all in politics, which was the passion of most of the more serious men in town. But Nicholas's lack of interest had been directly related to his feelings of powerlessness. Now he had position and financial security, and with these things, came a broadening of his own personal horizon. He was fortunate enough to meet for the first time a man with whom he had a great deal in common. At a party at Lady Cowper's, someone introduced him to the Earl of Linton, and the two men took an immediate liking to each other. Linton's estate of Staplehurst was famous for its successful and enlightened agriculture, and the two young men spent many pleasant hours in deep and thoughtful conversation. Linton was recently married himself, and Nicholas liked his wife very much. There was something about her that reminded him of Margarita.

Lady Eleanor Rushton was not in London, and Nicholas's visit was remarkably chaste. He went to a few routs and spent one rather pleasant night with a noble lady of doubtful virtue, but for the most part he worked. He was anxious to return home before the baby was born.

One of the reasons he went to the routs was that he wanted to meet Lord Castlereagh, the foreign secretary, and speak to him about the situation in South America. He was successful in meeting Castlereagh but the talk was discouraging. England was interested in South America solely as a profitable place to send its exports. The presently war-exhausted economies of Venezuela and New Granada lacked the means to buy, and therefore England was not very interested in rescuing them from the clutches of Spain. England's economy was distressing enough; she was clearly not going to spend the money to fight someone else's war.

"I had some very disturbing talks with Linton," Nicholas told Margarita that evening as they sat in comfortable chairs in the library. "Liverpool's government is pushing for a new corn law." At her puzzled frown he explained, "Import of foreign wheat will be forbidden until the price of British wheat rises above eighty shillings. It is protecting the British farmer at the expense of the British poorer classes. Linton says there will be famine if the law passes."

"But I thought England was a rich country," Margarita protested. "How can this be?"

"The government has a tremendous war debt to pay off. Also there are two hundred and fifty thousand demobilized soldiers and sailors who are looking for employment and most aren't finding it. During the war the economy boomed. Now we are paying the piper."

"I sometimes think that Christ must weep when he looks down on this earth and sees what we have made of it," Margarita said soberly. "There is so much suffering and most of it is due to man. Wars, people starving while food is being exported, babies dying for lack of care." Her face was somber. "I do not think Rousseau was correct, Nicholas. It is not only unjust political institutions that corrupt man. It is something in ourselves. Original sin, the Church would call it."

"Well, I, for one, have never erred on the side of high expectations when it comes to my fellowman," Nicholas said with a wry smile that did not touch his eyes.

Margarita sighed. "There is nothing to stop you from selling your corn for under eighty shillings, is there?"

The smile spread to his eyes. "No."

There was silence in the room. The rain was falling harder, and they could hear it drumming against the window. Margarita shifted in her chair as if she were uncomfortable, and Nicholas got up and went over to her, holding out his hands. "Bedtime for you, little one," he said briskly. "No more gloomy talk for tonight."

She took his hands and got to her feet. He looked down at her for a moment, appraisingly, as he had this afternoon. Aside from the bulk of her stomach, everything about her was so delicate and frail—cheek, ear, throat, wrist. Not for the first time a deep concern took hold of him as he thought of the approaching childbirth. He put his hands on her shoulders, carefully, gingerly, as if she might break if he gripped too hard. "Good night, Margarita." He gently kissed the top of her head.

"Good night, Nicholas." The eyes that looked up

at him were dark and soft and unspeakably beautiful. "I am glad you are at home," she said again.

He watched her walk to the door, and when she had gone sat down to stare into the fire, a painful line between his brows.

at him in the dark and
"I suppose you are about to—
She examined her words and—
had come far down until—
but hand on his brows were—

CHAPTER THIRTEEN

Season of mists and mellow fruitfulness.
John Keats

It was October. Catherine Alnwick had gone to London for a few weeks, and Nicholas refrained from riding into Chelmarsh to visit another widow-friend of his. He was apprehensive about being away from home and definitely felt guilty about pursuing his own illicit pleasure at such a time.

He took out a gun one particularly fine day, and when he returned home he discovered that Margarita had also gone out. Nicholas frowned in displeasure. He did not want her driving around by herself. She had been gone two hours. Nicholas sent to the stable for his horse and set out to look for her.

He did not have far to go. He was two miles from home, on what he knew to be one of her favorite paths, when he saw her coming toward him—on foot and leading the horse. He cantered toward her.

"What the devil do you think you are doing?" he asked, fright making his voice sound harsh.

"The wheel of the phaeton hit a stone in the road and broke," she answered. Her voice sounded a little strange, and he looked at her intently.

"Are you all right?"

"I've started having pains," she admitted.

He swore. "Where did you leave the carriage?"

"About two miles back. It can't be used, Nicholas. The wheel is badly broken."

"You weren't thrown?" he asked sharply.

She shook her head. "I was coming home because I had started to get pains in my back. I suppose I was not watching the road as closely as I should have, but nothing serious happened, as I was going very slowly. I unhitched Hero and started to walk." She stopped and he saw the muscles around her mouth tighten. He swore again.

"I never thought to take the other phaeton." He looked at his own horse. "Can I put you up on Cora, Margarita?"

"No!" She sounded breathless. "I will walk back."

So with two sets of reins in one hand and with his other arm supporting his wife, Nicholas undertook what he was certain was the longest two miles of his entire life. Margarita was obviously in pain, although she was making a gallant effort to hide it. They were spotted as they reached the bottom of the long drive, and servants came running to take the horses from Nicholas. He dispatched someone for the doctor and, ignoring her protests, picked Margarita up and carried her up the drive and into the house.

The woman whom they had hired as a baby nurse took over in Margarita's bedroom and Nicholas was banished. Margarita begged him to fetch Mrs. Frost, and after the doctor arrived, Nicholas did indeed drive his phaeton over to Whitethorn. Mrs. Frost was alone in the kitchen. "Of course I'll come," she said readily to Nicholas's question. "I promised your lady I wouldn't fail her and I shan't. Poor little thing, with no mother or sister or aunt to hold her hand and help her at a time when she most needs it." The farmer's wife took off her apron and disappeared upstairs for a few minutes. When she returned she had on her hat. "I'm ready, my lord."

When they arrived at Winslow, Nicholas accompanied her upstairs. At the door to Margarita's room, she turned and patted him kindly on the sleeve. "Don't fret, now, my lord. These things take time—especially the first. Just you try to relax."

She opened the door and went in. Nicholas heard Margarita's voice, breathless, as though in pain. "Mrs. Frost!" The note of relief in that cry was unmistakable.

"There, there, my lamb," came the farmer's wife's comfortable tones. "I've come to help you. Everything will be all right, I'm sure."

Slowly, Nicholas went back downstairs.

* * *

It did not in fact take long at all. Three hours

later a beaming Mrs. Frost knocked at the door of the library, where Nicholas had been pacing around like a caged tiger. "You have a son, my lord," she told him proudly. "A fine, healthy boy."

"A boy. How is my wife?" His voice sounded tense.

"She is fine. She did splendidly. And it was over so quickly!"

"Thank God," Nicholas said devoutly. "I don't mind telling you, Mrs. Frost, that I was worried. She is so small."

"I can say now, my lord, that I was worried too. But the baby is a nice size, and she delivered with no trouble at all. Dr. Macrae says you may come upstairs if you wish."

Nicholas started for the door with alacrity.

* * *

Margarita was sitting up in bed when he came into the bedroom. Her hair had been brushed and neatly plaited, and she wore a crisp white night dress. At the sound of the opening door, she looked up from the child in her arms and her eyes met Nicholas's. There was quiet in the room. He was aware of nothing but those great dark eyes fixed so steadily on his. Then she made a small movement toward the child in her arms. "Here is your son, my lord."

He crossed the room and looked down at the small bundle resting in the crook of Margarita's arm. The baby had downy brown hair and delicate, fair skin.

His eyebrows were amazingly well defined and Nicholas said, with profound surprise, "He has eyebrows!"

Mrs. Frost laughed. "Yes. And ten fingers and ten toes as well, my lord."

"He is perfect," Margarita said softly, her eyes on the baby's face. The child gazed back out of wide gray eyes. "His eyes will be brown. All my brothers and I had gray eyes when we were born."

"If he has eyes like you, little one, he will be a very fortunate boy," said his father. He held out a tentative finger and brushed it against the baby's cheek. "What shall we call him? We never talked of a name."

There was a note of surprise in her voice as she answered, "Nicholas, of course."

He looked at her. "I thought perhaps you might like to call him after your father."

"Antonio? No, Anthony would be the English." She smiled at him then, a lovely, warm smile. "That is very generous of you, my lord. Perhaps our next son. This one is Nicholas."

He felt absurdly pleased and was embarrassed by his pleasure. "If you insist," he said hastily. He took her hand. "I am so glad you are all right, little one. I was worried about you."

"It was painful but nothing I could not support," Margarita answered proudly. "In fact, Nicholas, I am very pleased with myself."

He laughed and bent to kiss her cheek. "And so you should be. Mrs. Frost said you did splendidly."

Margarita's small face glowed and Mrs. Frost said, "I think her ladyship should rest now, my lord."

Nicholas nodded. "Of course. Good night, sweetheart. I shall see you both tomorrow." She smiled and he went to the door, pausing to look back once before he left. She was still looking at him.

* * *

In the weeks following the birth of her child, Margarita became completely absorbed in the rich fullness of motherhood. She turned her sitting room into a temporary nursery so she could nurse the baby at night. They had hired a baby nurse to take care of him, but Margarita enjoyed the routines of dressing and bathing her son, and Mrs. Wade found herself acting more as a teacher than a doer.

Nicholas rather felt as if in gaining a son he had lost a wife. She was so immersed in the baby. Her life revolved around little Nicky: nursing, resting, bathing him, eating and drinking so her milk would be nourishing, nursing, resting again.

He missed talking to her. During dinner she told him about the baby, and after dinner she was so sleepy that he was sure she wasn't attending to what he was saying. He was impatient with her for being so tired and ashamed of himself for feeling impatient. He knew she was up at least twice during the night to feed the baby.

In spite of feeling a bit put out by the fuss he created, Nicholas was truly delighted with his son, especially as the weeks went by and the baby became more alert. He spent one fascinated hour observing the heroic efforts of little Nicky as he tried to get his hand into his mouth. And he became completely reconciled when he went into the nursery one afternoon at the sound of crying, picked the baby up, and the crying stopped. Tentatively he rocked the child in his arms and was rewarded with a beatific, toothless grin. Nicholas grinned back. Nicky was fine, as far as he was concerned. It was Margarita who was letting herself be overwhelmed by it all.

* * *

As the weeks went by and the baby grew and began to eat some strained food and sleep for longer periods, the physical demands on Margarita lessened and she began to turn once again toward Nicholas. By Christmas she was riding again, and in January she began to talk about redecorating the house. Nicholas, whose love for the castle was second only to his love for the land, was pleased by her ambition and told her not to worry about the expense.

If Nicholas had found her absorption in the baby irritating, he was finding the resurrected Margarita even more difficult to deal with. He had not approached her with anything even remotely suggestive of passion since last January, a year ago. First her sickness, then her advancing pregnancy had made it impossible for him to even consider forcing sex on her. She was perfectly healthy now, but still he hesitated. He was not afraid that she would reject him. He knew she would not. Margarita would never shirk what she considered to be her duty, no matter how unpleasant she might find it. And she *had* found it unpleasant. That was a truth he could not disguise from himself. Nor did she do anything that would indicate to him her willingness to resume relations. Never, when he kissed her cheek, did she offer him her lips. Never, when he put a casual arm around her shoulder, did she turn to him in a welcoming embrace. She treated him, Nicholas thought bitterly, as if he were her brother.

The problem was that he did not feel at all brotherly toward her. They were sitting in the library one evening after dinner when he asked her to play for him. She fetched her guitar, strummed it softly, then asked, "What would you like to hear, my lord?"

"Anything you like," he said, stretching his long legs toward the fire. "Something in Spanish." He loved to hear the soft liquid sounds of that language on her lips.

She tilted her head a moment in thought. Then she said, "There is a poem by Sor Juana Inés de la Cruz that I put to music for myself. The words are the words of a woman writing to her lover. 'My love, my lord,' she says, 'listen to my weary plaints awhile.' She misses him and longs to see him. All of nature, she says, is a reflection of her grief." Her fingers moved over the strings and she began to sing:

> *Amado dueño mio,*
> *Escucha un rato mis cansadas quijas ...*

Nicholas sat very still, his eyes on his wife. She

had a lovely voice, untrained but clear and true. The firelight cast a glow on her intent face. Nicholas looked from the profile of eyelid and lip down the shoulder and breast and bare arm. He watched the hand that was moving so expertly over the strings; the turn of wrist was so vulnerable in its white, veined fragility.

She had come to the last plaintive line: *"Regaré mi esperanza con mis ejos,"* she sang softly. The last notes died away, then looking up at Nicholas, she smiled. "Is that not lovely, my lord?"

A smile, reluctant and wry, flickered across his lips. "Very lovely, Margarita," he answered, with just a hint of weariness in the tones of his voice.

The next day he drove over to visit Catherine Alnwick who was once again in residence at Sothington.

CHAPTER FOURTEEN

He looked at her, as a lover can;
She looked at him, as one who awakes.
                        Robert Browning

There was one aspect of Margarita's character that Nicholas had not taken into consideration in his troubled state of mind. What he did not understand was her profound ignorance of anything sexual. She was a married woman. She had had a child. But when it came to passion she was no more than a child herself.

When she had first been married, all her senses were deadened, her emotions frozen. It had not been possible for her to respond to Nicholas as a lover. That situation no longer existed, but Nicholas, in his misguided consideration, made no effort to wake Margarita from her innocent aloofness.

Nicholas, distressed by what he thought of as his wife's frigidity, had no conception of the extent of her ignorance. English girls, though chaperoned and watched, had a freedom that was unheard of in South America. Margarita had never been to school. She had never giggled with her peers about beaux and love affairs. Until she married Nicholas she had never been alone with a man who was not closely related to her. She had never in her life even been to a dance. In most ways she was far older than girls her age, far more thoughtful and selfless and concerned. But sexually, she was still a child. She gave Nicholas no encouragement because she did not know how to. When he made no effort toward resuming marital relations, she thought it was because he did not want her to have another child too quickly and felt tenderly toward him for his consideration.

She loved him. He was the sun around which her life revolved. But she never thought she could show him that with her body.

* * *

In February, the three members of this particular lover's triangle were brought together for the first time in many months. The occasion was a dinner and dance given by Sir Henry Hopkins and his lady for a group of friends who had been visiting at Twinings. Margarita's game of whist had improved considerably, but Nicholas told her she would be expected to dance and not to play cards, and she had to confess that she had never learned to dance.

He was astonished. "Well, yes, I can see that the

dances in Venezuela may have been somewhat different from ours, but surely you learned *some* dances."

Margarita shook her head. "You must remember, Nicholas, that I was fifteen when my mother and brother Antonio died in the earthquake. Caracas was virtually rubble; it was not a city inclined to hold dances. Then in July, Miranda surrendered Venezuela to Monteverde. My father and I went to San Pedro and my brothers left the country. They had been officers in the Republican army, and Monteverde would have had them executed. The next year the war began again. There was no time for me to learn how to dance."

He looked in silence at her earnest face. His mouth was hard and straight and unsmiling. "I see."

She looked a little anxious. "Perhaps I could learn in time for the party?"

In response, he reached out and gathered her close to him for a minute. "Of course you can learn, little one," he said over her head. "I'll teach you."

She closed her eyes for a minute and rested her head against his shoulder, happy and safe in the warmth of his arms. With a slow and almost stealthy movement, his cheek came down against her hair. Then he straightened. Gently, but very decidedly, he put her away from him.

* * *

Margarita proved an apt pupil, and when they arrived at Twinings for dinner, she was secure in the knowledge that she would not disgrace Nicholas when it came to dancing.

The houseparty consisted of Lord James Tyrrell, who took every opportunity he could to see Margarita, Colonel and Mrs. Leigh, Mr. and Mrs. Underwood and their seventeen-year-old daughter Louisa, and Lord and Lady Alvin and their son George. Lady Hopkins had invited the Winslows, Mr. Knight and Lady Anne, Catherine Alnwick, and Dr. Macrae and his wife to meet them.

Margarita went in to dinner with Sir Henry and conversed with him and with Lord Alvin, who was on her other side, with a sweet gravity they both found most beguiling. Sir Henry had become very fond of young Lady Winslow and had expressed himself with unaccustomed force to his wife about Nicholas's notoriously discreet affair with Catherine Alnwick. The whole neighborhood wondered if Margarita knew about it. No one, of course, would ever be crass enough to question her, and no sign of trouble had ever creased her serene oval brow at the sight of her rival. What Margarita knew and what she thought remained a mystery.

After dinner they went into the drawing room, where the furniture had been pushed back and a small orchestra installed. About twenty other people from the area arrived, and the dance began.

Margarita danced the first dance with Nicholas. As he stood beside her waiting for the music to begin, he glanced down, his eyes resting on the smooth curve of her cheek. She turned a little and smiled, looking up at him with brown eyes full of innocence and trust. The dark storms rose within him. He did not want it from her, that childlike innocence. But he was afraid to puncture it, perhaps only to replace it with fear. It defeated him, that look. The music started and he led her into the dance.

The crisis for Margarita happened about halfway through the evening. There was a break in the music as they were waiting for the next set to be formed. Margarita was standing with Lord James Tyrrell, who had claimed her hand. She glanced around, instinctively, to locate Nicholas and saw him standing by the chimney piece, his posture casual, almost disdainful. Her eyes traveled past him and lit on Catherine Alnwick. Catherine, too, was watching Nicholas. Her eyes were slightly narrowed, and there was an expression on her face that caught and held Margarita's attention. As she watched, Catherine crossed the space that separated her from Nicholas. He saw her coming, leaned his shoulders back against the mantel, and waited. She put a light hand on his arm and said something. He looked down at her, his eyes hooded, the ghost of a smile on his lips. Then he took her elbow in his hand, and they moved together toward the supper room.

There was an air of unconscious intimacy about them that hit Margarita like a blow. She stared after the brown and blonde heads that were disappearing toward the supper room, and as she watched, Catherine slipped her hand through the crook of Nicholas's arm.

"Lady Winslow?" said Lord James Tyrrell.

"Yes?" she replied, as if accosted by a stranger.

"The music is starting," he pointed out, and blinking as if she had just awakened, she gave him her hand.

After the dance, Lord James took her in to supper. Nicholas and Catherine were still there, and Margarita moved to join them. Her husband instantly arose when he saw her, and Catherine smiled a perfectly natural welcome, but nothing in the subsequent half-hour of general conversation could dispel the impression Margarita had received earlier. The image of Mrs. Alnwick and her husband, associated in unconscious familiarity, stayed with her, like something detected, a scene illuminated by a sudden flash of lightning.

* * *

In the days immediately following the party at Twinings, Nicholas noticed a change in Margarita. Once again she seemed to have retreated from him. She did not physically withdraw her presence; rather it was as if she had gone away within herself. He asked her two or three times if anything was the matter, but she always replied in the negative.

In fact, Margarita was struggling with unfamiliar and frightening thoughts. For the first time in her life, she was jealous. She thought back over the past year with Nicholas and began to realize that what Nicholas did not get from his wife he most likely got somewhere else. Catherine Alnwick's tall slender figure, her blue eyes and patrician face, were constantly before Margarita's eyes. She saw again and again those eyes, narrowed with possessive desire, looking at Nicholas.

Four days after the dance, Margarita came into the library to retrieve her needlework, which she had left on the worn leather chair that stood in front of the fire. Nicholas was there, lounging comfortably in the other leather chair, his eyes on a book that was propped on his knee. He did not hear the door open, and for perhaps half a minute she stood in the doorway, studying his half-averted face. It was a face as familiar to her as her own, yet now she looked at it as if for the first time, seeing the gray-green, long-lashed eyes, the flat, finely shaped ears, the thick brown hair that looked so boyish above the strong column of his neck. The faint hollow under the cheekbones. The arrogant nose and straight, firm mouth.

She had married Nicholas at a time when every physical feeling had been battered out of her. She had seen him first as an enemy and later as a friend; never had she seen him primarily as a man. He looked up and she was struck, blindingly, by the vivid male force of that suddenly, strangely unfamiliar face. She flushed.

He rose from his chair. "Were you looking for me?"

She went straight to her needlework. "I only came for this." She refused to look at him, her eyes resolutely downcast.

He looked with puzzlement at the profile of privacy he had not seen on her for almost a year. A sense of *déjà vu* came over him as he remembered a similar scene in this same library about a year ago. Something had happened; he knew it, but he didn't know what it was. "Margarita?" he asked.

She turned to him, her dark brown eyes withdrawn and guarded. She could find nothing to say. He took a step nearer. "Has something happened?"

She shook her head. "Of course not. I must feed the baby, Nicholas. He has been cutting a tooth, I think." She seized on the excuse. "I am just a little tired, I suppose. Nicky hasn't been very happy these last few days." She stepped backward. "I will see you at dinner." With a relief she carefully tried to conceal, she turned and left the room.

CHAPTER FIFTEEN

O that 'twere possible
After long grief and pain
To find the arms of my true love
Round me once again!

Tennyson

For the first time since her marriage, Margarita began to consider the nature of her relationship with Nicholas. Like an animal awakening from a long winter's hibernation, she looked with newly opened eyes at the scene that surrounded her, and for the first time she found it strange.

Why did Nicholas never make love to her? It was the question that plagued her night and day. He had come to her often enough in the first weeks of their marriage. It was only after she became pregnant that he had ceased visiting her room, and since the birth of Nicky he had not returned.

She did not please him. He did not find her attractive. This was the only conclusion she could come to. He had done his duty until she had conceived. Now that he had an heir he did not need to approach her again. He could continue his affair with Catherine Alnwick: tall, cool, blonde, English Catherine. Margarita hated her with a primitive jealousy she had not thought it was possible to feel. She wanted to fight Catherine for Nicholas, but she did not know how to do it. She did not know what to do to attract him. The thought crossed her mind that perhaps she could make him jealous of *her*, but it was a short-lived idea. Margarita had never resorted to cunning in her life; it had never been necessary to be anything other than what she was. She didn't know how to begin to change.

* * *

It was a bitterly cold day at the end of February. Margarita was undressing for bed. It was late, after midnight. Nicky had been fretful with the tooth he was cutting, and she had spent the evening rocking and singing to him. Finally he had gone to sleep, and she had come into her own room to undress. Her maid, Chute, was waiting for her. Margarita smiled at the woman absently and cast a glance at the door that connected her room to Nicholas's. The crack of light under the door told her he was still up.

Chute began to unbutton Margarita's gown, turning away once or twice to sneeze. "Are you getting a cold, Chute?" Margarita asked. "You needn't have waited up for me, you know."

"I am all right, my lady," Chute answered somewhat nasally, holding out Margarita's nightgown. When the nightgown was on and the dressing gown over it, Margarita sat at the dressing table and Chute brushed out her hair.

"That will be enough," Margarita said when it was falling free and shining to her shoulders. "Go to bed, Chute. And stay there tomorrow if you feel unwell."

"Yes, my lady," the dresser said thankfully. She put the brush down on the table, and as she did so her body was seized by a violent sneeze. Her hand jerked and the brush crashed against a bottle of perfume, knocking it over and breaking it. Margarita jumped up in haste and Chute cried out.

Nicholas was standing in front of his bedroom window, looking out at the frozen night, when he heard Chute's cry and the sound of something breaking. He belted his dressing gown and went into Margarita's room. The first thing that hit him was the overpowering scent of perfume. Chute was babbling hysterically and trying to mop up the dressing table, while Margarita spoke soothingly, saying everything would be all right.

"What a reek!" Nicholas said humorously, and both women started at the deep sound of his voice.

Margarita met his eyes and her dimples flickered. "Isn't it dreadful? I never liked that perfume, even in small amounts, but now . . ." The heavy, sweet odor was overpowering. Chute repeated apologies.

"Never mind it now," Nicholas said authoritatively. "The room will have to be aired, and it can't be done tonight. You can sleep in my room tonight, Margarita. The fire is blazing and it's nice and warm." She came slowly across the room toward him, wrapped in a rich velvet robe, her hair hanging loose down her back. He frowned. "Is there glass on the floor? Watch out you don't cut your feet." She looked down and trod carefully.

"Go to bed, Chute," she said over her shoulder. "The maids will attend to it in the morning."

"Yes, my lady," the woman replied faintly. She sneezed. "Good night, my lady, my lord."

"Good night," Margarita said firmly and closed the door behind them.

Nicholas's room *was* warm, although not as warm as hers. "Get under the covers and I'll put another log on the fire," he told her. She obeyed him, taking off her robe and climbing into the huge four-poster. When he turned around she was sitting up, straight-backed and still, her huge brown eyes watching him warily. He thought he knew what that look meant.

"You should be comfortable enough here," he said a little wearily. "I'll get one of the maids to make up another room for me."

Margarita felt as if he had struck her. He couldn't even bear to be in the same room with her. With her breath almost a sob in her throat, she scrambled out of the bed and stood barefoot on the cold floor. "Nonsense. If you don't want to share a room with me, then *I* shall be the one to leave. There is no point in both of us being put out of our beds."

"Don't be ridiculous," he said sharply. "There is no fire in any other room. You'd freeze."

She shook her head, wordless, and went back to the bed to get her robe. Nicholas, finally, understood that he had hurt her. He hesitated, then went to stand next to her, feeling huge, his eyes on her averted face. He put his hands on her shoulders and turned her to face him. "I am not going to sleep here tonight because I couldn't share a bed with you and trust myself to keep my hands off you. It is as simple as that."

His hands were hard on her shoulders, biting with unconscious strength into the soft flesh. Margarita felt her heart begin to thud as his words registered in her mind. He seemed to be saying that he *did* want her. She took an uneven breath, looked fixedly at the lapel of his dressing gown, and spoke in a low voice. "I thought you did not find me pleasing."

There was a stunned silence, and then Nicholas said quietly, "Don't you ever look in your mirror?"

She was afraid to look at him. Gently, his arm came up around her, and she rested her head against the lapel she had been regarding so intently. Under her cheek, his heart was hammering. Those hammer beats gave her the courage to lift her head. "Don't go," she said.

"Are you sure?" His voice sounded oddly breathless and she nodded gravely. He cupped her face in one of his hands, bent his head, and slowly began to kiss her. She stood very quietly and his hand slid from her cheek up into her hair. He had himself under rigid control, conscious of the stillness of her lips under his. Then, very slowly, her mouth opened for him, and with a tentative sweetness that took his breath away, she began to kiss him back.

Without releasing her lips, he lifted her in his arms and carried her to the bed. He lay her back against the pillows and with clumsy masculine fingers, began to undo the buttons of her nightgown. She let him do them all and, when he had finished, raised her arms like a good child so he could pull it over her head.

Her body was as beautiful as he remembered. The only change was in her breasts, which were no longer small and pointed. He ran an exploratory finger down the curve of one of them. "Did you really think I found you not to my taste?" he asked incredulously.

"I did not know what else to think." His finger had left a trail of white fire behind it and she gazed at him, a mixture of apprehension and dawning passion in her dark eyes.

He took off his dressing gown and got into bed beside her. His mouth twisted a little as his eyes ran over the bared perfection of her body. "You are the most beautiful thing I have ever seen or am likely ever to see," he said huskily, and then his mouth claimed hers once again. His hands moved gently on her, so delicate, so sure. He was being very careful. He could not bear it if she stiffened against him.

But she didn't. At first she was very still, neither giving nor withholding, but as the passion rose in him, an answer awoke within her and she melted for him, flowered and opened, soft and silken and infinitely beautiful under his love.

Afterward, she looked at him in wonder, her face a little flushed. "That was wonderful. I loved it. Why didn't I like it before?"

He shifted a little above her, afraid his weight was

too much for her. His breathing was finally slowing. "You weren't ready, little one," he said. "You were grieved and afraid and hurt. I should never have touched you."

Her brown head nestled against his shoulder and he drew her close against him. "Nicholas *mío*," she whispered. "*Mi vida, mi amor.*"

He stiffened slightly, hearing those words. He had never felt so close, so one with a woman, but old fears flickered nevertheless. She said nothing more, and precisely because she had not asked, he felt he had to be honest. "Margarita," he said a little harshly, "don't ask me for love. If I care for anyone in this world, it is you, but love . . ."

She didn't answer for a moment, but he felt the sweep of her lashes against his bare flesh. When she finally spoke, her voice was warm and soft, gentle and reassuring, the voice she often used to Nicky. "It is all right, Nicholas *mío*. I have enough love for both of us." She said no more, and after a few minutes he could tell by the deep evenness of her breathing that she had gone to sleep. It did not take him very long to follow suit.

CHAPTER SIXTEEN

There is none like her, none.
Tennyson

She awoke with the dawn. The room was frosty, but under the covers, lying close to Nicholas, she was warm and comfortable. She closed her eyes and savored the closeness of him, the weight of his hand on her. He woke soon after she did. She felt his arms slip around her waist, pulling her closer. He put his mouth on the nape of her neck. Everything inside her quivered and melted at his touch, and she turned to him with welcoming, yielding passion. When she shifted a little beneath him so he could come deeper, he said in a voice she could hardly recognize, "Almighty God."

Two hours later she heard the sound of someone making up the fire. After the maid had left, she sat up. He reached a lazy arm and pulled her down again, but she strained against it. "Mrs. Wade will be bringing Nicky to me to nurse any minute now. She'll wonder whatever happened to me."

"Stay where you are," he said. "I'll fetch Nicky." He rose, stretched before the fire like a giant cat, and put on his dressing gown.

"You might hand me my nightgown first," she murmured.

He picked it up. "Do you need it to nurse the baby?"

"I need it if I am going to sit up in this drafty room. It buttons down the front."

He quirked an ironic eyebrow at her but forbore comment about what he felt was her hypersensitivity to cold. He handed her the nightgown and went out into the hallway. They had moved the baby into the third floor nursery ten days ago, and he went down the hall to the back staircase that led directly to Nicky's rooms.

He was back in his own room in ten minutes, a yelling baby in his arms.

"Here's your son," he said to Margarita, unceremoniously handing over the indignant Nicky.

"He's hungry, that is all," said Margarita with amusement. Once Nicky discovered that his needs were about to be answered, he broke off abruptly and addressed himself with gusto to the matter at hand. After a moment, Nicholas came back to the bed, his eyes on the steadily sucking baby at Margarita's breast. He bent toward them a little, and looking up, Margarita's head touched his. She smiled at him, radiantly beautiful, fulfilled and content. Looking at her, he felt curiously humble; he did not deserve to be looked at like that.

* * *

The days went by, and the only shadow on Margarita's happiness was the recurring nightmares that stemmed from her experience in Venezuela, and even they were growing fewer and less intense. Nicholas was afraid to say that he loved her, but Margarita had no doubt that he did. He said it in his lovemaking, he said it in the way he watched her face when they were together, he said it in his smile. Margarita had been surrounded by love all her life. She thought she knew what it looked like.

She thought she knew also the reason for Nicholas's reticence. The only real quarrel she had ever had with him had been over her determination to write to his mother.

"I do not want you corresponding with her, Margarita, and that is final," he had said in a tight, controlled voice.

"No, it is not final, my lord," she replied calmly. "When a woman becomes a grandmother, she has a right to know. I do not ask that you write. You are angry with her and I accept that, although I do not approve of it. *I* will write. It will be nothing to do with you."

She remembered vividly the look that came over his face—black, bitter pride shutting down over anger and hurt. "*She* is nothing to do with me. Or with you either. Do you understand me?"

She drew herself up to her full height, her chin in the air, the breeding and arrogance of Spain momentarily stamped on her lovely face. "Yes, I understand you, my lord. I understand that you are an unforgiving, cold, heartless man. And what is more, I think you are afraid." She stared at him steadily as he towered over her. "Now are you going to give me her address or do I have to get it from your man of business?"

He gave her the address and she had written. She received a reply to her letter but kept it to herself. Neither she nor Nicholas ever referred to the subject again.

*　*　*

In March, she gave a party. Andrés Bello had come to Winslow for a visit, bringing with him another South American, Juan Vicente Montilla. Montilla was in Cartagena throughout Morillo's long siege and was fortunate enough to escape after the city fell in December. He joined Bolívar, who was now in Haiti. "The Haitian president, Alexander Pétion, has promised to assist Bolívar in a new expedition," Montilla told them that first evening, as they sat over coffee in the drawing room. "Many of the men who succeeded in escaping from Cartagena have found their way to Haiti—Mariño and Brion are there as well. President Pétion has agreed to provide ammunition to the expedition."

"How many men does Bolívar have?" Nicholas asked.

The Colombian looked a little rueful. "That is what your government officials keep asking me, my lord. He has over two hundred men, but there will be ammunition for thousands. South Americans will rise for him, you will see."

"Two hundred men against one of the greatest expeditions ever sent out by Spain?" Nicholas looked incredulous.

"It will not be two hundred men," Margarita put in passionately. "Don Juan is correct when he says South Americans will rise for Bolívar. They will rise for freedom."

Both American men nodded gravely. Nicholas found the faith they all displayed in this Simón Bolívar rather frightening and at the same time very moving. "He must be quite an extraordinary man, Simón Bolívar," he said slowly, and the other three looked a little surprised.

"But of course," said Margarita. "He is *El Libertador*."

* * *

It was in order to entertain her guests that Margarita organized a dinner party. Invited were Sir Henry and Lady Hopkins, Mr. Knight and Lady Anne, Dr. and Mrs. Macrae, and Catherine Alnwick.

For one reason or another, Margarita had not done very much entertaining, and she was anxious that everything should go smoothly. She was anxious, too, at the thought of meeting Catherine Alnwick. She had never so much as hinted to Nicholas that she knew anything of his affair. She did not want to hear about it, to hear him explain it. It happened before he had come to her, and now it was over. That was all she cared to know. She never for a moment doubted that it was over.

The evening went very well. The American men made a favorable impression on everyone, and Catherine Alnwick made a distinctly strong impression on Juan Montilla. He shared his countrymen's appreciation for blonde hair, which was seen but rarely in his native land, and Catherine's type of fair, English beauty attracted him strongly. In a perfectly polite fashion, he devoted himself to her, thus according great, if unspoken, relief to most of the remaining company. Nicholas, who had not been to see her in weeks, was feeling slightly guilty and uncomfortable. The Hopkinses and the Knights, who knew through the servants' grapevine about his defection, were afraid the evening might prove to be rather strained and were happy to see her safely occupied. Margarita was as gracious and charming and shyly friendly as ever; no one could detect any difference in her manner to the beautiful Mrs. Alnwick.

The gentlemen did not linger over their wine, and when they joined the ladies, Catherine was at the piano. She played very well: she did most things very well, and Margarita was listening with genuine pleasure when the door opened and the men came in. Nicholas's eyes sought his wife immediately, a fact noted with satisfaction by the vigilant Lady Hopkins.

Catherine Alnwick was coaxed to play again, and

then Lady Anne sang an Italian song in a well-trained soprano. "Do you play, Lady Winslow?" Catherine asked sweetly, and Margarita shook her head.

"My father went to great lengths to get a piano for my mother. She was a very fine musician, but I fear her talent was not passed along to me. I play very badly."

"You have another instrument," Nicholas said quietly, and Andrés Bello leaned forward in his chair.

"I took great pains to find you a good guitar, *niña*, and I expect to hear it." When she flushed and hesitated, he said softly, "Please. It is so long for me."

She capitulated instantly. "Of course I will play for you, Andrés."

Nicholas spoke to one of the servants and the guitar was brought. Everyone sat quietly, curious and interested. Margarita looked at Andrés Bello. "I set a poem of Quevedo's to music. I did it in our home in Caracas, just before the evacuation." Her eyes moved to her husband's attentive face. "It is a sad song," she said. "A lament, you would call it. The singer says that the walls of his country are in ruin. The countryside is dark. His house is falling down. Everything about him reminds him of death." She bent her head a little and began to play:

> *Miré los muros de la patria mia,*
> *Si un tiempo fuertes, ya desmoronados,*
> *De la carrera de la edad cansados,*
> *Por quien caduca ya su valentia.*

Salíme al campo, vi que el Sol bebía
Los arroyoys del yelo desatados,
Y del monte quejosos los ganados
Que con sombras hurtó su lux al día.

Vencida de la edad sentí mi espada,
Y no hallé cosa en que poner los ojos
Que no fuese recuerdo de la muerte.

There was a haunted, brooding note in her low voice that conveyed the meaning of the song even to those who knew no Spanish. The last word died away and Margarita sat still, her downcast eyes on the strings of her guitar. Then she looked up, looked at Andrés Bello, and Nicholas, silently and to himself, cursed. He recognized all too well the expression on her face.

Andrés Bello answered her look. "I know, *niña*," he said very softly. "But you must have the courage to build again, the courage for the long climb back to happiness. We all must have that, or what is to become of us and of our country?"

Juan Vicente Montilla, who had completely forgotten Catherine Alnwick, now said with rigid lips, "We will do it or we will die trying."

Sir Henry cleared his throat a little, uncomfortable amid the sudden outburst of Latin emotions in the room. Margarita looked at him and realized what had happened. He was a nice man, she thought to herself a little blankly. They were all nice people. But they were all a little unreal, a little childish, unaware of the terrible shadow of chaos that constantly threatened the frontiers of life in this world. But they were her guests. She must not discompose them. She forced a smile.

"I will play one more song for you, a song that was my father's favorite. It is about a man who goes out to catch a fish for his dinner and what befell him." Her fingers moved over the strings. The tune was catchy and sprightly, and after the first two verses, Andrés Bello joined in with her. By the time the song was over they were both laughing a little, and the tense, embarrassed feeling had vanished from the room.

As she was taking her departure, Catherine Alnwick announced to her host and hostess that she was leaving for London in a few days.

"Will you be staying long?" Margarita asked.

"For the Season, I expect. I go every year." This was true, but Catherine did not usually go in March. Nicholas, however, forbore to comment on the change in her routine.

"We shall miss you," Margarita said serenely. "My lord speaks of our going to London as well. Perhaps we shall see you there."

Catherine smiled brilliantly. "Perhaps. Goodbye, Lady Winslow, Lord Winslow. It was a delightful evening."

"Good evening, Mrs. Alnwick," Nicholas said gravely. "I wish you a good journey."

His feeling of guilt over Catherine had only increased by seeing her this evening. He knew very well that he could not break off their relationship without some kind of an explanation. One did not summarily dismiss a mistress, who had given satisfaction for five years, without so much as a word. At least, Nicholas could not.

He forgot about Catherine, however, as soon as he got upstairs. Margarita was standing by the window, her back rigid, and he knew, without seeing her face, that she was crying.

"Andrés Bello was right, little one," he said to that straight back. "You do have the courage to fight back to happiness."

"Yes," she replied and her voice sounded muffled. "Sometimes I do. But sometimes I feel as if I haven't changed at all, that time is frozen inside of me and it is all happening over and over again, and I shall *never* forget it and never get over it." She turned then to face him, and he could see the tears pouring ceaselessly down her face.

He came across to her and picked her up. At that moment, her dresser came to the door and he frowned ominously, causing the woman to back away in fright, almost slamming the door behind her. He sat Margarita down on the bed and undressed her with gentle hands. "I can't stop crying," she sobbed, and he pulled off his coat and shoes and swung into bed beside her.

"I know," he said, "but try. You'll make yourself ill if you keep on like this."

His shoulder was so familiar, so safe and secure. She pressed her face against it and he held her against him. Slowly her sobbing slowed and ceased, and she slept.

CHAPTER SEVENTEEN

How the light, light love, he has wings to fly
At suspicion of a bond.

Tennyson

By mid-March, Margarita was deeply involved in plans for redecorating Winslow. The project involved a great deal of self-education on her part, for English architecture and furniture design were completely unfamiliar to her.

"The furniture in my father's houses was all modeled on the designs of the Spanish Renaissance," she told Nicholas at the start of her project. "The lines of that style are all rectangular and straightforward. There is nothing even remotely resembling *that*." She gestured with incredulity toward a chair that was one of Chippendale's more exotic Chinese efforts.

Nicholas had grinned. "I see what you mean."

"We have beautiful wrought-iron work in our houses, for another thing. You have nothing like it at all here. It is a completely different kind of architecture and decoration from what I am accustomed to. I shall have to learn about English styles."

"Would you like to re-do the house in the Spanish style?" Nicholas asked curiously.

She did not hesitate. "No. It would not look right in this house. Spanish furniture is for a southern climate. Although"—and nostalgia glimmered in her eyes—"I would not be at all unhappy to find a few pieces of authentic sixteenth or seventeenth century Spanish furniture. My father had the most beautiful *vargueño* . . ." Her voice trailed off.

"What is a *vargueño*?" Nicholas asked after a half-minute of silence.

She smiled. "It is a kind of a desk. My father had one that his grandfather brought from Spain. It had the most beautiful ivory inlay you have ever seen."

Nicholas mentally determined that he would scour the earth until he found an ivory-inlaid *vargueño* for her. But all he said was: "I am afraid I'm not going to be much help to you. I can tell you the different periods of most of the furniture, but the fine points of decoration and design are not my forte. Perhaps we should get a professional in."

"Not yet," she answered. "I want to be more knowledgeable before I do that. Lady Hopkins has promised to help me, and perhaps you and I can start by just looking carefully at what we have."

Cataloguing the house's furniture was not very difficult. There were a few pieces of the original Jacobean furnishings, but the majority of things were Queen Anne and early Georgian, with a great preponderance of Chippendale. "I don't think my uncle ever touched the house," Nicholas told Margarita. "His father, my grandfather, had Mr. Chippendale re-do all the state rooms and I suppose he thought that that sufficed. However, that was fifty years ago. I don't even think all the rooms have been painted since then."

"Good heavens," Margarita said faintly. "What was the reason for such monumental neglect?"

Nicholas looked sardonic. "Your grandfather couldn't see the point of putting money into something that would one day only go to a nephew. I think the neglect started when he didn't have a son of his own."

Margarita's lips were unusually severe. "How can that be? He spoke of Winslow to me with great affection. He was proud of its ancient history, of its being named in the *Doomsday Book*."

The sardonic look vanished as Nicholas shouted with laughter. "The *Domesday Book*, sweetheart, not 'Doomsday.' "

"*Domesday*, then," she repeated. "But he truly sounded as if he loved Winslow, Nicholas. I don't understand."

"He loved it so much he hadn't set foot in it for thirteen years."

"Thirteen years!" There was profound surprise on her face.

"He stayed at Winslow for as long as my aunt lived; she did not like the city. But as soon as she died he moved to London and never returned."

"I don't understand," she repeated in bewilderment.

He gave her an odd, slanting look from under his lashes. "Why do you think he forced you to marry me the way he did?"

Her eyes were steady and grave on his face. "He wanted to provide for me, of course."

"He could simply have left you the collection. Why did he tie your future to me?"

His voice was expressionless. It was impossible to tell what he thought. "He wanted to be sure there would be someone to take care of me," said Margarita.

He looked at her for a moment in silence. She was speaking what she thought was the truth. And he thought that, given her background, it was the natural conclusion for her to draw. One of the first priorities for all her men had always been to make sure there was someone to take care of Margarita. He was sorry now he had brought the subject up. "Why do *you* think he made his will the way he did?" she was asking him.

"You probably have the answer," he replied easily. "He wanted to be sure you were looked after."

"But that doesn't explain his neglect of Winslow," she went on. "Or why, after so many years, he decided to return."

He shrugged. "It hardly matters, now," he said. His face wore a look of complete indifference.

Her thoughtful brown eyes never left his face, registering every flicker of expression on it. She came to the answer more by intuition than by reason. "You think he wanted me at Winslow, don't you? *I* was his grandchild, and you were not. That was why he was coming back here after so many years. And that was why he made *you* marry me. Was that it?"

"Yes," he said.

She felt a deep anger within herself, anger at the man who had been so brutal, who had hurt Nicholas so badly. There was a tight feeling in her chest. No wonder, she thought, he was so guarded against love. She wanted to throw her arms around him and comfort him but his face warned her not to offer sympathy. She drew an uneven breath and turned and walked to the window so he would not see the tears in her eyes. "He must have been a very stupid man," she said lightly. "However, his stupidity has made me very happy so I cannot complain too loudly."

He came across to where she stood and put his hand on her neck, beneath her hair. "Has it made you happy, sweetheart?" he murmured.

She leaned back against him. "Yes," she said, and his hand moved forward over her throat and in between the buttons of her dress.

"Good," he said, and bent over her.

* * *

They planned to go to London at the beginning of April. Margarita pored faithfully over the copies of Sheraton's *Cabinet Maker and Upholsterer's Drawing Book* and *Cabinet Dictionary* that Lady Hopkins lent her. She looked carefully through Thomas Hope's *Household Furniture* as well and she made some basic decisions about what she wanted to do. She planned to redecorate the family rooms first and see how they came out before she tackled the more formidable state rooms. Lady Hopkins recommended that she commission George Smith to make the furniture for her, and she decided it would be easier for her to go to London since she would then be able to look at fabrics for drapes and walls as well.

Nicholas was going to take his seat in Parliament. Lord Linton had written to tell him that there was an important bill coming up, and Nicholas promised to be there for the debate and the vote. He also wanted Margarita to look over the large number of remaining paintings. They needed to decide what to keep and what to sell.

All was in train for their departure when Nicky got sick. He had a cough and a fever. Dr. Macrae came and said it was the same influenza that had struck half of the houses in the neighborhood. He didn't seem to think it was serious, but of course it was impossible to take a sick baby on a journey to London, and Margarita, who was still nursing him, couldn't leave him even if she wanted to.

"You go ahead, Nicholas," she urged him. "You promised Lord Linton you would be there for the vote. Nicky isn't seriously ill. I can manage here very well without you. And as soon as he is better, I'll join you in London."

She was very firm and in the end he gave in and left without her. That was at the beginning of April. After a week she wrote to tell him Nicky was completely recovered but that Mrs. Wade had taken ill. "I really need her to help me with Nicky on the journey," she wrote, "so I am going to wait until she is better. I hope your introduction to Parliament went well."

The next communication Nicholas received from Winslow came from Mrs. Wade. Margarita had come down with the same influenza that had felled both Nicky and herself. "Lady Winslow begged me to tell you not to return to Winslow," the nurse wrote. "She says you will only come down with influenza yourself and she would prefer to have you healthy. As soon as she is recovered she will join you in London."

In the end, it was May before the Winslow family was reunited in Berkeley Square.

CHAPTER EIGHTEEN

So darke a mind within me dwells
   And I make myself such evil cheer
That if *I* be dear to someone else,
   Then someone else may have much to fear.
                              Tennyson

For the first week of his sojourn in London, Nicholas was involved with the Parliamentary session. Escorted by Lord Linton, he took his seat and was introduced to nearly all the leading Whig politicians. He was most cordially received. The Beauchamps, as befitted one of the most ancient families in the country, had always been relentlessly Tory and tended to regard with disdain Whigs like the Romneys of Linton, whose titles dated only from the time of Queen Elizabeth.

Nicholas was not ready to declare himself a Whig, but neither had he any use for the Tory government of Lord Liverpool. In Philip Romney, Earl of Linton, he found a kindred spirit. Linton was only a few years older than Nicholas, but they had gone to different schools, and as Nicholas was rarely in London, their paths never crossed until last year. The two men had taken an instant liking to one another, each man recognizing in the other a sympathy of thought, and Nicholas was sorry when Linton left London to return to his home in Kent.

"My wife is expecting a child next month and naturally I don't like to be away from her for long," Linton said to Nicholas. "Perhaps this summer you and Lady Winslow might pay us a visit at Staplehurst."

Nicholas accepted with genuine pleasure.

* * *

The departure of Linton left Nicholas with time on his hands. He was besieged by invitations, as the Season was getting under way, and as he found the empty house getting on his nerves, he attended more parties than he had any real desire to attend. He missed his wife. And, inevitably, he ran into Lady Eleanor Rushton and Catherine Alnwick.

Lady Eleanor and he had been lovers in an off-again on-again fashion for about two years. In fact, Nicholas had not seen her for almost a year when he met her at Lady Palmer's reception. In ten minutes Lady Eleanor made it perfectly clear that as far as she was concerned, his long absence made no difference. "My husband is still in the country," she murmured, large green eyes glinting up at him. "Why don't you escort me home tonight?"

His first impulse was to say No. He had no real desire to resume his affair with Eleanor Rushton. He hesitated, searching for the words to tell her so. "Or have you turned into a good and faithful husband?" she said, amusement in her rich voice.

His response was uncalculated and automatic, his hand coming up to rest, caressingly, on her bare shoulder. They were standing in an alcove of Lady Palmer's ballroom and were unobserved, as they thought. Lady Eleanor put her hand over his for a minute, and laughed.

"When I think of the money most of us have spent on women over the years and I look at Winslow, I could cry," said Lord Melville to Lord James Tyrrell. They had both been watching the byplay between Nicholas and Lady Eleanor.

"What do you mean?" Lord James asked, constraint in his voice.

"I mean that he hides himself in the country for most of the year, yet the minute he appears in London, half of the most desirable women in town are ready to lie down for him. And it was that way when he was only Nicholas Beauchamp, with hardly a guinea in his pocket. He's probably never spent more than twenty-five guineas on a woman in his life," said Lord Melville disgustedly.

"No, I suppose not." There was an unaccustomed line between Lord James's brows.

"He didn't bring his wife with him, I notice," said Lord Melville.

Lord James drew himself up. "Lady Winslow stayed at Winslow with her son, who was ill with influenza. I understand she will be coming to town shortly." He gave Lord Melville a very frosty nod and moved away.

Lord James was not happy, and it was not his own lack of success with Lady Eleanor that was disturbing him. He wanted to tell Nicholas that he was a fool for wasting his time on Eleanor Rushton, but he did not have the nerve. *He* was not enough of a fool to provoke Nicholas's temper. He thought of his friend's temper, of his mistresses, of his occasional hair-raising adventuring, and then he thought of Nicholas's wife. The more Lord James thought, the more profoundly unhappy he became.

*　*　*

Nicholas was not overly happy with himself. He had not intended to let himself become involved with Eleanor Rushton again. It was her provoking taunt about his being a good and faithful husband that had done it. Something in him needed to prove, not to Eleanor Rushton but to himself, that he was *not* tied like that to Margarita. The problem was that he missed her damnably, and the more he missed her the more he sought to demonstrate to himself that he was perfectly capable of living comfortably without her. So he got himself embroiled with Eleanor Rushton and, when he visited Catherine Alnwick to end their affair, with her as well.

*　*　*

Meanwhile, at Winslow, Margarita was struggling

with fatigue, illness, and depression. She missed Nicholas dreadfully. Without him everything was such an effort. And every time she thought she was ready to leave for London, something else happened to delay them. First Mrs. Wade got sick, along with half the staff. Then the whole burden of looking after Nicky fell on Margarita, and she was exhausted from toiling up and down stairs, carrying him around, feeding him, cleaning him, amusing him, and all the time trying to soothe the sensibilities of servants who were not feeling well and were working, like she, at jobs they were unaccustomed to.

There was no one to share it with. She missed, almost more than anything else, Nicholas's shoulder. It was the small things, she discovered, that brought home to her most acutely his absence. The unimportant, everyday things: the light touch on the cheek, the hand that rested so casually on the nape of her neck, his shoulder to lean against when she was tired and depressed. She had woven the new fabric of her life about those things. They represented to her peace and security and deliverance from loneliness. Without them she was adrift and lost.

She was worn out, which was why she fell so sick with the influenza. It was two weeks before Dr. Macrae would allow her to get up and another four days before she was able to get into the coach to begin her trip to London.

It rained the whole way. Nicky was cranky and fussed almost constantly. He was learning to get his legs under him so he could push himself up on all fours, and he did not like the confinement of the coach. He did not want to be held. He did not want to nurse. He just wanted to get out of the carriage. By the time they stopped for the night it was only three o'clock in the afternoon, and Margarita was almost in tears.

They reached London in the late afternoon of the next day. Margarita, carrying Nicky, ran up the stairs under the shelter of an umbrella held by a footman. Reid was in the hall. "Welcome, my lady. I hope you did not get wet."

"No, thank you, Reid," she said, shifting the burden of Nicky from one shoulder to another.

"Here, give that great lug to me," a voice said, and Nicky was efficiently plucked from her arms.

"Oh, *Nicholas*," she cried thankfully, the intensity of her relief causing her to abandon for once the careful formality she always maintained in front of others.

He had an arm around her, and she leaned her forehead for a moment against his shoulder. When she straightened up, her eyes were brighter than they had been in weeks. "I was beginning to think you had deserted me," he said, and she shook her head vigorously.

"Never."

* * *

The efficient, healthy Berkeley Square household took charge, and soon Nicky was happily trying to stand on his head in his crib, and Margarita was sitting down to dinner with Nicholas. She had lost weight, and there was a sallow tinge to her skin and shadows under her eyes—and Nicholas thought that she was the most beautiful thing he had ever seen. He made her drink two glasses of burgundy with him, which brought some color to her cheeks. He listened sympathetically to her tale of woe, then told her about his own experiences when he took his seat in Parliament. They sat over dinner for almost three hours and Margarita was looking much less tired at eleven than she had at eight.

They left the dining room and went right upstairs to bed. "Nicholas *mio*," she breathed as he got in beside her. "How I have missed you."

"And I you," he returned, his hands moving over the remembered perfection of her body. She opened for him, like a flower to the sun, and he came into her without delay, his eyes closing as he held her close. The peace of being with her again. It was only Margarita who could do this for him. They moved together in perfect unison.

For Margarita it was sheer heaven, being with Nicholas again like this. When he said, afterwards, his cheek against hers, "There is nothing in the world as good as this," she sighed with contentment.

"I love you," she said softly.

That night, curled against the security of Nicholas, she slept more soundly than she had for a month.

CHAPTER NINETEEN

O never talk again to me
  Of northern climes and British ladies.
                    Byron

The first thing Nicholas did was to take Margarita out and buy her a whole new wardrobe. They went to a very exclusive shop in Bond Street that Nicholas had heard recommended by Catherine Alnwick. Margarita protested when she realized the amount of money Nicholas was prepared to spend. "I am sick of seeing you in that everlasting black," he said firmly. "And the dresses you had Mrs. Burgess make at Winslow will not do for London. If I run out of blunt I'll simply sell another painting."

Madame Fentôn had been thrilled to have the young Countess of Winslow for a customer and had known exactly the styles and colors that would most suit her dark-eyed, delicate-boned beauty. Margarita and Nicholas left the shop laden down with boxes and Madame Fentôn promised to send those that needed alteration to Berkeley Square later in the week.

The Duchess of Melford was giving a ball three days after Margarita's arrival, and Nicholas thought that this would be an auspicious occasion for introducing his wife to the ton. The ball would be one of the greatest crushes of the Season, and Margarita would have an opportunity to see most of the people who mattered in London society without, herself, being the center of interest. Many women would have relished a more spectacular entrance into society, but his wife, Nicholas knew, was not one of them.

Margarita was nervous but she made a gallant effort to disguise her apprehension from Nicholas. She had very little experience with large parties and was not sure how the evening would proceed, but, as she told herself prosaically, the only way to find out would be to go.

Nicholas's eyes lit up when he saw her, and she knew that she looked well. She wore a gossamer gown of shell-pink gauze with a scooped neckline that showed off the astonishingly delicate loveliness of her throat, shoulders, and arms. Her hair was drawn smoothly off her face and dressed in a heavy knot on the top of her head. A few tendrils had been allowed to escape and fall artistically about her neck. Nicholas put her cloak carefully around her shoulders. "You look beautiful, sweetheart," he said encouragingly. "Pink suits you."

She turned to look at him. "And you look very handsome, my lord." She inspected his neatly brushed hair closely and then gave a little nod of approval.

He grinned. "I got it cut this afternoon."

"It looks very nice," she said sedately, and they went out together to the coach.

There were carriages lined up for almost a quarter of a mile outside the Duke of Melford's house in Grosvenor Square. They had to wait in the carriage for half an hour before their own vehicle drew up before the splendidly lighted entrance of Melford House. Once they were inside, they went up the staircase to the wide landing where the duke and duchess were receiving their guests. "The Earl and Countess of Winslow," the majordomo intoned, and Margarita found her hand being taken by a tall, aristocratic lady of indeterminate middle age, who peered at her curiously and said, "So you are Winslow's wife. Very happy to meet you, my dear. I do hope you enjoy yourself. It promises to be a sad crush, I fear."

"Thank you, Your Grace," Margarita said softly; she smiled a little stiffly, murmured something to the duke, and let Nicholas escort her into the ballroom.

It was a huge, elegant room and it seemed to her to be filled with people. "Do you *know* all of these people?" she asked Nicholas in bewilderment.

He laughed a little. "I know some of them, little one. I doubt if even the duchess knows them all." The music struck up and he took her hand. "Will you favor me with a dance, Lady Winslow?"

She smiled at him warmly. "Of course, my lord."

After the dance was over, Lord James Tyrrell materialized by their side, and with Nicholas's approval, he took Margarita to the dance floor. When he brought her back to Nicholas there were several people waiting to be introduced to her, and someone else took her out to dance. Upon her return this time, there was a familiar face waiting next to Nicholas. "Cousin Lucy!" exclaimed Margarita. "I did not know you would be here."

"I didn't realize *you* were in London, or I would have called on you. How lovely to see you again, my dear. You look wonderful."

"Thank you." Margarita nodded gravely. Then a dimple flickered. "You must come and see Nicky. He is growing so big. Just like his father."

"I hope he's not *too* like his father," Lady Moreton said dryly. "One of him is more than enough."

Margarita's chin rose a trifle. "I hope he is just like my lord," she said firmly. Over her head Nicholas's eyes met Lady Moreton's, and it was he who looked away first.

* * *

Margarita found the evening a bewildering parade of faces and names. She felt very foreign and very shy, but she was determined not to let Nicholas down and forced herself to smile and make conversation. It was difficult. The conversations were all brilliant surface with no substance, and Margarita found herself drifting away on a shimmering sea of patter. She tried, with only limited success, to catch onto a lifeline of reality. She had a few moments of interesting talk with Mr. Canning about Spain and a delightful, short conversation with Lord Holland about Cervantes. The rest was vapor.

Nicholas watched her progress with satisfaction. She was so lovely, so grave and sweet and fragile-looking, that the men to whom he introduced her were instantly charmed. And she favorably impressed the women whom it was important she impress: Lady Jersey, Countess Lieven, Mrs. Drummond Burrell, the Duchess of Melford.

"Margarita is making a decided hit," said a voice from over his shoulder in unconscious echo of his own thoughts, and Nicholas turned to look at his cousin, Lady Moreton. He looked back at his wife, who was dancing with Viscount Debenham. "Yes," she said. "She is."

"She is so young, Nicholas. And so fragile."

Nicholas knew what his cousin was saying to him and he answered obliquely. "Look at Margarita dancing, Lucy. Do you notice her back?"

"Her back?" repeated Lady Moreton in puzzlement.

"Her back. It was one of the first things I noticed about Margarita." He looked around at his cousin. "Solid steel, Lucy," he said, an expression in his eyes that Lady Moreton had never seen before.

"She has been through a great deal, of course," Lady Moreton replied slowly.

"She is probably one of the few adults in the room," he answered. His mouth twisted a little. "Myself included."

* * *

Both Catherine Alnwick and Eleanor Rushton had been at the Melford ball, and both had been decidedly piqued when Nicholas failed to dance with them. Eleanor Rushton, in particular, watched his careful chaperonage of his wife with displeasure. She was not pleased, either, with Margarita's appearance. It did not add to her happiness to discover that Nicholas's wife was so attractive.

Other people were delighted by Nicholas's neglect of his mistresses. Lord James Tyrrell was one, and Lady Moreton was another. Lady Moreton called on Margarita the day after the Melford ball and was initially pleased by what she found. From Nicholas's behavior the last month, his cousin had deduced that his marriage was not notably successful. It seemed she was mistaken.

Margarita received her graciously in the impressive, picture-filled drawing room of the Beauchamp town house. "You look very lovely, my dear," Lady Moreton said appreciatively, casting expert eyes on Margarita's fashionable walking dress of dark gold. "I am glad to see you did not rely on the wardrobe I purchased for you last year."

"My lord said he was tired of seeing me in black," Margarita explained. "He took me to Madame Fentôn's in Bond Street and bought me *far* too many clothes." Margarita looked faintly disapproving. "It was very expensive."

If Nicholas purchased a whole new wardrobe for

his wife at Madame Fentôn's, it must certainly have been expensive, reflected Lady Moreton. She looked curiously at Margarita. "Well you look perfectly splendid, my dear. The money was well spent."

"It gave my lord such pleasure, you see," said Margarita simply.

There was a little silence as Lady Moreton digested this information. "And you, also," she said finally.

"Of course," replied Margarita, but Lady Moreton got the distinct impression that Margarita's satisfaction derived not from the clothes but from her husband's pleasure in buying them for her.

They went upstairs to see Nicky, and Lady Moreton was suitably full of admiration. Over tea, Margarita confided to her cousin her ambition of redecorating Winslow, and Lady Moreton volunteered to accompany her to Mr. Smith's in Cavendish Square.

Nicholas came in as Lady Moreton was on the point of leaving. He stopped to say a few words to her, and out of the corner of her eye, she watched Margarita watching her husband. She loves him, she realized in surprise. Her eyes went back to Nicholas's smiling, arrogant, handsome face. His kind of sophisticated carelessness was alien to the innocent sweetness of a girl like Margarita, Lady Moreton thought. She held out her hand in farewell, and as Margarita took it, Lady Moreton looked closely at her. Her eyes were dark pools of serenity. Suddenly, Lady Moreton was afraid for her. It was dangerous for a woman to love Nicholas like that.

CHAPTER TWENTY

The little rift within the lover's lute,
Or little pitted speck in garner's fruit,
That rotting inward slowly moulders all.
                              Tennyson

At first, Margarita did not at all like the social whirl of London's famous Season. She found it difficult, even painful, to talk to people she did not know and did not care about. She was taken aback as well by the frivolity and immorality of many of the people she met. They had no understanding of the seriousness of life, she found herself thinking far too frequently. They were like careless children who vandalize out of boredom and out of ignorance. Margarita had too great a sense of the precariousness, and consequently, the preciousness of life to be able to enter into their games.

Nicholas could join in better than she, but that was because he had other reservoirs to draw on, and for him society was only a diversion. And, too, at every dinner and every ball, he always found someone to talk to seriously, in the direct, uncomplicated, yet technical way of men. Margarita all too often was left listening to empty compliments and talking to ladies, about fashions she had no interest in and about the scandalous behavior of people she did not know and did not approve of.

Gradually, however, and whenever he could, Nicholas would include her in his conversations, and Margarita found herself discussing agriculture and foreign policy and reform and manufacture and books and art. She did not understand everything but she listened carefully, and when she did venture to speak, she was listened to with courtesy and interest. "Very thoughtful girl, your wife," said Lord Bingley to Nicholas one evening. "Sensitive. Aware." He nodded approvingly and Nicholas felt absurdly pleased and proud.

* * *

By the beginning of June, Margarita had found herself a comfortable circle of friends. She did not have a gregarious nature and would never be a leader of the ton, but that was a position to which she did not aspire. She hadn't the patience for it. She was content to have found a congenial group of friends and was far more inclined to put her energy into the few people she liked, and was in sympathy with, than spread herself more thinly.

She saw quite a bit of Andrés Bello, and it was at a reception that she attended with him that she met Captain Williams once again. The captain had heard of her marriage and frequently wondered how she was faring as the wife of that intimidating, handsome young man he had met so briefly four years ago. He was delighted to see her again, and delighted to see her looking so well.

They discussed, of course, the news from South America. Bolívar had landed on Margarita Island, and Arismendi and his followers had risen for him. An assembly of notables convened and recognized Bolívar as the supreme chief of the Republic. Bolívar's next aim was the mainland. The two men discussed at length the prospects of success for the Republicans, and Margarita remained a silent auditor. Her emotions were so tied up with the topic that she could not speak temperately and objectively. All she could say was that they *would* win because they *must* win. For her father, for her brothers, for all the thousands and thousands of men, women, and children who had already died. They must win. Any other result was unthinkable.

Nicholas had promised to meet her at the reception and he was late. She had been looking for him for half an hour when he finally came in, making all the other men look small. He caught her eye and came across the room. She introduced him to Captain Williams, and Nicholas laughed ruefully as he remembered their own previous meeting together. Captain Williams, confronted with all the humor, charm, and vigor of Nicholas at his best, rapidly reassessed his opinion of Margarita's husband.

Margarita felt less tense as soon as Nicholas arrived. She listened to the sound of his voice and watched the play of expression on his face. After a bit she joined the conversation, and shortly after that Nicholas took her home.

They did not talk about it, but the evening had been a strain on her and Nicholas knew it. Captain Williams brought back to her so much of the past. Just when she thought she had gotten her life on an even keel, something always seemed to happen to remind her that beneath the smooth waters of the present lurked the terrible, the fearful, the unbearable. It seemed, at these times, that only Nicholas could save her from drowning in those memories. He was comfort and understanding, peace and strength. She thought over and over again that night of how much she loved him.

* * *

Lady Eleanor Rushton was very angry indeed. Nicholas had wounded her heart a very little bit and her vanity a great deal more. She had never before been cast in the role of discarded mistress and she was furious. Nicholas simply avoided her. She had contrived to be introduced to Margarita by one of the more malicious ton hostesses, but Margarita quite clearly had no idea who Lady Eleanor was. And since Margarita instinctively shied away from the people for whom gossip was the breath of life, apparently no one had as yet told her. Eleanor, casting around for appropriate vengeance, determined that she would be the one to shatter Margarita's innocence.

Once she decided upon this course of action, Eleanor did not delay in carrying it out. Her opportunity came at a ball given by Lady Jersey. With ruthless thoroughness, Eleanor stepped on the hem of Margarita's gown and tore it. Then, gushing apologies, she insisted that the girl come with her and let her pin it up. Margarita agreed.

Eleanor congratulated her on having such a satisfactory husband. She called Nicholas by his first name. She laughingly said that Margarita must be a wonder, to have held him faithful for a month now. She said the men—wretches that they were—were betting in the clubs as to how long he would keep it up. She left no doubt at all that she and Nicholas had been lovers. She mentioned other names as well. One of them was Catherine Alnwick.

Eleanor was quite satisfied with her evening's work. When she left Nicholas's wife, Margarita looked white and shocked and shaken. She had not given Eleanor the satisfaction of any reply. She simply said, in a tight little voice, "Go away from me, please." But her face gave her away.

It took Margarita quite a few minutes to school her expression to stillness. She felt nauseated. She felt unclean. She felt betrayed. When she finally went back into the ballroom, she looked for Nicholas. He was dancing with Catherine Alnwick.

* * *

Catherine had been out of London for a few weeks visiting friends in Warwickshire. When Nicholas saw her at the Jersey ball, he made up his mind to talk to her. As far as he was concerned, their affair was over, but he knew that she deserved an explanation. So he asked her to dance. And asked if he could call on her later in the evening. She agreed to both requests.

He escorted Margarita home in the carriage and told her he had promised to meet a friend at Brooks's for a late drink. They were in the hallway, with the night footman looking on, and she said stiffly, "Very well, my lord. Good night." She turned away before he could kiss her.

He returned to the carriage and gave Catherine Alnwick's address. Margarita's behavior struck him as odd, but he didn't dwell on it. Most of his attention was focused on his coming interview and what he would say to Catherine.

* * *

She received him in the drawing room. When Nicholas, led by Catherine's butler, found her waiting for him, still dressed in her ball gown, he knew that she was going to make it easy for him. A surge of affection for her rose in him. He kissed her hand and smiled down at her. "I like you very much, Cat. You have always been a good friend."

Her answering smile was a little strained, but she smiled. "This is goodbye, I presume."

He looked at her cool, lovely, aristocratic face. "I hope we can continue to be friends," he said seriously. "But lovers—no."

He was still standing, and she rose now and walked restlessly to the fireplace. "It is your wife, of course," she said, staring into the flames.

Nicholas had expended much thought on how to present the situation to Catherine. He could hardly tell her that he had no interest in any other woman when Margarita was around, that she gave him something he got from no one else. It was the truth and the main reason Nicholas had found to account for his unusual faithfulness. However, it would be less than tactful to say that to Catherine. So he gave her, instead, the other reasons he had invented to satisfy himself as well as her. "Margarita had a very bad time, Cat. She lost her entire family in the Venezuelan war. I am her family now and she depends on me. I can't let her down. And I owe her something, too. After all, she gave me my son."

Nicholas watched as Catherine slowly turned to face him. He was himself very satisfied by his explanation. It made excellent sense, he thought. Catherine regarded him thoughtfully and he looked steadily back. "It would upset your wife to discover that you had been unfaithful?" she asked.

That was a subject upon which Nicholas had no doubts. "Yes," he said.

"Then if I were you, I should keep her away from Eleanor Rushton."

He frowned. "What do you mean?"

"I mean that I saw her leave the room with Lady Eleanor this evening and then come back later by herself. It must have been Eleanor's doing. I doubt if your wife would have made the suggestion of a tête-à-tête. Eleanor is hardly her style."

Nicholas's eyes narrowed. "If she has upset Margarita, I'll murder her," he said, icy rage in his voice.

Catherine's blue eyes never left his face. "You love her, you know," she said neutrally.

His face was taut. The eyes looking back at Catherine were inimical. Part of him knew that what she said was true, that he did love Margarita. But the part of him that was still scarred by a seventeen-year-old desertion refused to admit it. "Nonsense," he said harshly. "I feel responsible for her, that is all."

"Well, if you feel responsible for her and you don't wish her to discover your, ah, peccadilloes, then I suggest that *you* keep away from Lady Eleanor as well, Nicholas." There was a white line around his mouth, and Catherine's eyes softened as she watched him. "Poor boy," she said sympathetically, "you have gotten yourself into a tangle."

"I know I shouldn't have started that up again," he said stiffly. "But, damn it, Cat, Margarita was away for over a month! I'm not a bloody monk."

Catherine looked amused. "That is one thing you have never been accused of," she agreed.

"Margarita will just have to understand about these things." He sounded decidedly autocratic.

She raised an eyebrow. "Will she?"

"Yes," he said. "She will."

After he left, Catherine walked slowly up the stairs to her solitary bed chamber. She had always been perfectly satisfied with her life, she thought.

Nothing major had really changed. She would miss Nicholas, of course, but, philosophically, she had not expected their relationship to continue forever. There were other men in the world. Why, then, did she feel so inexplicably sad?

TWENTY

CHAPTER TWENTY-ONE

I might have known,
What far too soon, alas! I learn'd—
The heart can bind itself alone,
And faith may oft be unreturn'd.
Matthew Arnold

It was a very uneasy and disturbed Nicholas who walked back to his own house at three o'clock in the morning. He let himself in, as he had told the night footman not to wait up for him. He did not expect anyone to be waiting in his bedroom either, as he had told his valet to go to bed, but there was someone there, seated in the big fireside chair. It was his wife. She was dressed in nightgown and robe and had a blanket tucked around her. She looked up as he came in and shut the door behind him. "Where were you?" she asked.

"What are you doing up?" he returned. "It is after three in the morning!"

"I know." Steadily she repeated her question. "Where were you?"

He regarded her thoughtfully. "I told you I was going to Brooks's."

"I know you did. I don't think I believe you." She was very pale and her eyes were enormous.

"Where do you think I went, then?" he asked quietly.

"To your mistress. To Mrs. Alnwick." She put up a hand to tuck the blanket more tightly about her, and he saw it was shaking. He sighed and went to sit in the chair opposite to hers.

"Margarita," he said gently, "whatever was between Mrs. Alnwick and me has nothing to do with you. It has no effect on my feelings for you, believe me."

"That was what I thought," she replied, a slight quiver in her voice. "I thought it was all over. But I see now I was wrong."

"What did Eleanor Rushton tell you?" he asked grimly. The question itself was an admission.

She wouldn't look at him. Her voice was so low he could hardly hear it. "She told me that you had many mistresses. I would not have minded that so much if they had all been *before* you and me. But she told me you . . . saw other women . . . this last month, when I was not here."

Her head was bent. Nicholas looked at that small brown head and felt savage rage against Eleanor Rushton. He cleared his throat. "You must understand, Margarita, that a man has certain needs. You were at Winslow for over a month!" He repeated the line he had used to Catherine Alnwick. "I am not a monk, after all."

Margarita was not amused. She raised her head and looked very steadily at Nicholas. "No," she said. "You are not a monk. You are my husband."

He was finding it difficult to sustain that clear, brown gaze. "What do you want me to do?" he asked, his feet moving restlessly on the carpeted floor.

What she wanted was reassurance. She wanted him to promise her never to touch another woman again. Above all, she wanted to be told he loved her. But she could not extract any of those things from him because he felt guilty and uncomfortable. They had to be freely given. She sat in silence for a long minute, hoping, but nothing came. Finally he spoke, his voice now quick and hard with exasperation. "Don't just sit there looking like a tragedy queen. I tell you those women mean nothing to me. You are my wife. You are the mother of my son. That is all that matters." Then, as she continued to sit silent, "Margarita!"

"That is not how my father treated my mother," she said quietly.

"This is England," he responded curtly. "We do things differently here."

"Yes, I have found that out. I thought we were different, you and I, but I see now I was mistaken." She rose from her chair, and even in her night robe and clutching a blanket, she managed to look dignified. "Very well, my lord, since that is your wish, we will have an English marriage. I have, according to your custom, done my duty by you. I have given you a son. In future you will be perfectly free to do whatever you choose to do. I will expect, however, that you leave me alone." She walked to the connecting door between their rooms, went through, and locked it behind her.

Nicholas's mouth fell open. He shook his head a little dazedly and went to try the doorknob. He shook it. "Margarita!" he shouted. "Open this door! Now!"

There was no reply. He looked speculatively at the door and tentatively put a shoulder against it. Then he stepped away, a very grim look around his mouth. He could break through if he wanted, he had no doubt about that, but he could not do it. There had been too much violence in Margarita's life. He could not add to it. He would frighten her half to death if he came crashing through that door into her room.

He went back to sit in the fireside chair, stretched his legs out in front of him, and spent the rest of the night staring despondently at the carpet.

* * *

Margarita did not sleep either. She did not cry, but lay awake, feeling that a heavy weight was pressing down on her chest. She wished desperately that she hadn't gone to Lady Jersey's ball, hadn't talked to Eleanor Rushton. Last night she had lain here in Nicholas's arms. Last night she had thought he loved her.

For Margarita, Nicholas's behavior could mean only one thing. He did not love her. She had thought he did. She thought love was behind the caresses, the lovemaking she found so ecstatic. And now she knew that he did the same things with other women. Said the same things to other women. It was as if the bottom had dropped out of her life. All the security and faith and peace she had found in him were destroyed. Nothing in her life would ever be the same again.

* * *

At first Nicholas did not think that Margarita would hold out long against him. With all the enormous charm he could summon up when he wanted to, he set himself to woo his wife. He met with a solid wall of resistance. She managed, with a skill that he remembered from the first months of their marriage, to largely avoid being alone with him. And when he did manage to get her by herself she would look at him watchfully and edge toward the door, like a captive anxious for escape. All the warmth and glowing life was gone from her face. In its place was the still, guarded look he remembered too well.

There was nothing he could do, short of forcing himself on her, and that was impossible. The only times she was her old self were when she was with Nicky. Nicholas came into the nursery one afternoon to find her sitting on the floor playing a peek-a-boo game with the baby. Nicky was chuckling excitedly and Margarita was laughing along with him, cooingly, soft and gentle, deep down in her throat. Nicholas's face lit with pleasure at the sight and sound of them, but when she looked up and saw him, all the joy died out of her eyes.

He did not know what to do to break through to her. She had given him his freedom, but he did not again make the mistake of turning to another woman. All of London was convinced that the young Winslows had a very solid marriage. In fact, those friends who were closest to them were in no doubt at all that Nicholas truly loved his wife. The problem was that this pleasant conviction was not shared by either of the two parties most closely concerned.

* * *

Margarita was profoundly unhappy. The dark cloud created by Lady Eleanor's cruel words was constantly with her, making everything black and wretched around her. She walked through her days in blank misery, knowing there was nothing to be done, there was no place of consolation to be found. She was not angry at Nicholas. The desolation she felt did not permit any room for such a vibrant emotion as anger. And she knew she could not blame him for her despair. He had told her not to ask him for love. It was she who had allowed herself to believe he loved her, she who had depended on him, unfairly, for all that was meaningful in her life. No wonder now he looked at her in bewilderment and hurt. But she could not help the way she felt. She could never turn to him with confidence again.

* * *

On June 20, Lord and Lady Winslow attended a party given by the Regent at Carlton House. Nicholas had made plans to return to Winslow with his family, but those plans were disrupted by the Regent's unexpected invitation. One did not refuse a request to attend a party at Carlton House, particularly if it was the first time one had been invited, and so the Winslows delayed their departure and Margarita bought a new dress. Nicholas was not overjoyed to have his plans upset. He was anxious to get Margarita back to the country, where he hoped things between them would return to a more normal state.

On the evening of the party, Margarita appeared in an Italian silk gown of pale lemon yellow. It was sophisticated and stylish, and along with the diamond tiara that added to her height, it lent her courage. She had never been to Carlton House and never met the Regent, and she felt distinctly apprehensive.

The imposing, brilliantly lit portico of Carlton House was extraordinarily impressive. The Winslows were directed by masses of footmen to proceed through the hall, which was lined with Ionic columns of brown Sienese marble, and more footmen bowed them up the graceful double staircase to the Chinese Room.

Margarita's eyes were huge. She had never seen anything like Carlton House before. "Versailles could not be more magnificent," she whispered to Nicholas, and he cocked an eyebrow in agreement.

There were over a thousand people present, and the dancing had already started in the Chinese

Room when the Winslows arrived. They stood together for a minute, looking on and seeing very few people under the age of forty.

"You don't want to dance, do you?" Nicholas said. "Let's explore."

For the first time in weeks her dimples appeared. "Yes, let's," she said. And so husband and wife wandered off by themselves to investigate the marvels of the Regent's palace. It was marvelous indeed. The supper table was set up in a conservatory that looked like a cathedral, with Gothic pillars, tessellated ceilings, and marble floor. Margarita was entranced by the tropical plants and exotic flowers, many of which she recognized from home.

They moved on from the conservatory to other rooms, stopping to admire exquisite pieces of furniture from France, Gobelin tapestries, magnificent Sèvres china, and marble busts by Coysevox. In front of a lovely landscape by Claude, they met the Regent himself.

Nicholas was surprised when the Regent recognized him immediately. "Winslow!" he said, warmly shaking him by the hand. "I'm glad to see you here. I hope you are going to give me a chance to buy some of your uncle's paintings."

Involuntarily, Nicholas grinned. So that was the reason for the invitation. He had wondered. "Of course, Your Royal Highness," he answered. "My wife and I will keep some of them, but I certainly plan to put a large number up for sale."

"Splendid. You must let me know which ones you

are selling. There are a number of paintings I am particularly interested in."

"I shall certainly do so, sir."

The Regent smiled at Margarita. "You may present your wife to me, Winslow."

"Your Royal Highness, may I present Lady Winslow," Nicholas said obediently, and Margarita, glancing at him fleetingly, curtsied.

The prince made a few pleasant remarks to her, and she replied in the low voice she used when she was feeling shy. She was not sure how to address him, felt embarrassed and wished he would stop talking to her and go away. The Regent was pleased by her delicate loveliness, apparently didn't mind her obvious shyness, and after a few more minutes took himself off, leaving a relieved husband and wife behind.

The remainder of the party was easier. They returned to the Chinese Room where they met several people they knew. Margarita danced a number of times and had a very pleasant conversation with Lord Bingley about the Spanish painter Velasquez. They had supper in the Gothic conservatory and took their departure at about one-thirty in the morning.

"Well, we brushed through that pretty well, I thought," Nicholas said, as they were waiting for their carriage.

"Yes, except I was so embarrassed talking to the prince. He had to bend way over to hear me!"

Nicholas chuckled. "He didn't look as if he minded." He was feeling good. Margarita had not been this relaxed with him for weeks. They had drawn together, rather as children do when they are surrounded by adults, and the camaraderie still lingered. He handed her into the coach and then got in beside her.

As soon as he was seated, she froze. All the innocent fun of the evening was erased from her mind and she was acutely conscious of him, of how close he was, of how much she loved him. She stared straight ahead, afraid that he would touch her.

Nicholas looked at her remote profile and swore silently. His hands clenched themselves into fists, but Margarita did not notice. She was too occupied with staring at the wall of the coach.

CHAPTER TWENTY-TWO

> And most of all would I flee from the
> Cruel madness of love.
>
> Tennyson

When they reached home, Margarita went upstairs to bed. She was suddenly very tired and gratefully let her maid undress her and brush out her hair. "Good night, Chute," she then said. "Thank you."

"Good night, my lady," the woman replied and left the room. Margarita got into bed and snuggled down under the covers. She did not check to see if the door that connected her room to Nicholas's was locked. It was not.

Nicholas spent an hour drinking brandy in the library before he came upstairs. He never liked his valet to wait up for him, so he was alone in the bedroom, taking off his shirt, when his eyes were drawn, as if by a magnet, to the door that led to Margarita's bedroom. With sudden decision, he went over and tried it. To his surprise, it opened.

Very quietly he entered her room. There was no sound from the bed, and he crossed the floor and stood looking down at his wife. She was deeply asleep, lying on her back with her face turned away from him, one arm thrown back above her head. The light from the dying fire illuminated her pale cheek and the long, straight, childlike lashes lying on it. Before he had time to think about the wisdom of what he was doing, Nicholas got into the bed beside her.

Margarita was dreaming that she was in Nicholas's arms and he was telling her he loved her. "Nicholas, *mio*," she whispered and opened her eyes to find him there beside her.

"You forgot to lock the door," he muttered, and went on doing what he was doing. Her breath caught in her throat. She knew she should tell him to go away. He moved his hand to her stomach and felt the ripple deep within her. "Margarita." It was almost a groan.

It was too late to send him away. She would die if he left her now. There was a wildness in the way she clung to him, in the way she answered to his own desperate, driving need. It was hungry, urgent lovemaking, and its intensity surprised both of them.

He lay for a long time with his face buried in her neck, but she made no effort to put her hand up to smooth his hair. At last, he raised his head. Gently, he kissed her eyelids. "A man would be a fool to go elsewhere when he can get this at home," he said.

She could feel his strength, the warmth of his

body. She closed her eyes. "Is that a promise to be faithful?"

He laughed softly. "If I can have you, I'll stay faithful. Surely that sounds fair?" He moved his mouth across her throat. "Don't be jealous, little one. Believe me, you have no cause."

Long after Nicholas had gone to sleep, Margarita lay curled up in her corner of the bed, trying not to cry, trying not to toss or turn, to lie still and rigid and quiet so as not to wake him. How could he have done this to her? How could he have used the power of love to so humiliate and outrage her? She loved him and so she was vulnerable to him. This would happen again and again. There was nothing she could do to stop it. Except . . . Toward dawn, a thought began to take shape in her mind and at seven o'clock she finally fell asleep.

* * *

Nicholas was gone when she awoke at ten thirty. In the sunlight of reality her plan of last night looked impossible. To leave Nicholas—how could she do it? How could she accomplish it? She lay back against her pillow trying to think rationally, to think like a man, to think like Nicholas. What would she need?

Money. She got out of bed and went over to the small French desk near the window. She opened the drawer and took out the money she had put there. It was pin money, Nicholas had said when he gave it to her. She was to spend it on anything that took her fancy. She had bought some toys for the baby, but otherwise hadn't touched it. Nicholas had paid all her clothing bills.

She counted it. There was over a hundred and fifty pounds.

She drew a deep, uneven breath. She would need to hire a carriage. She couldn't take Nicholas's carriage to run away from him in. Reid would know where she could hire one. Reid knew everything. She would get dressed and have Chute pack her one portmanteau. She would have Mrs. Wade pack Nicky's things. Then she and Nicky would get into the hired carriage and leave. It sounded very simple.

Reid was deeply alarmed by Margarita's request that he hire a post chaise for her. He suggested several times that she take the Winslow coach. Finally, she put on her most imperious, Spanish manner and he went away to do as she requested. But first he sent a footman around to White's with a note for Nicholas.

The post chaise was at the door a little after noon. Margarita and Nicky got in. The Berkeley Square household was in a state of utter consternation, but no one knew what to do. Reid had been sending footmen all around town trying to locate Nicholas. He had not been successful. No one had the least idea where Margarita was going. Mrs. Wade was on the verge of hysterics.

Nicholas arrived home at five o'clock to be met at the door by a very disturbed Reid. "My lord!" that sorely tried retainer cried with uncharacteristic warmth. "I have had footmen all over town this afternoon looking for you."

"What has happened?" Nicholas's brows snapped together instantly.

"Perhaps I have been precipitate, but I was a trifle alarmed as I had not been informed," Reid said in a troubled voice. "Lady Winslow requested that I hire a post chaise for her this morning and she and little Lord Selden left in it at about noon today."

"Left?" Nicholas said blankly.

"Yes, my lord."

"Where did they go?"

"I do not know, my lord."

"Jesus . . ." Nicholas turned from the butler and went upstairs. Margarita's room was empty. He went into his room and saw, propped upon the chimney piece, a folded white piece of paper. He picked it up and read:

My Lord,

I know it is a very great sin for a wife to leave her husband, but that is what I have done. It is impossible for me to live with you at this moment. I must have time to try to think, to try to understand how I best can live in the future. I will try very hard to come back, but I do not know if I can.

I have taken Nicky as I could not leave him. I know you will be worried and I will write as soon as I am settled. I am going to someone who I think will understand.

This is not your fault. The fault is in me.

Margarita

Nicholas sat, white-lipped, staring at the piece of paper. He couldn't take it in. She had gone. He read the note again. What had happened? He looked toward her room and then he remembered. Last night. But she had *responded* to him. He hadn't raped her, for God's sake.

He started pacing around his room. He had to bring her back. God knew what would happen to her. Alone. His blood ran cold at the thought of her stopping at an inn by herself.

He picked up the note again. "I am going to someone who I think will understand," she had written. Who? She knew hardly anyone in England.

Immediately, the name flashed into his mind. Mrs. Frost. Of course, he thought, with a wild rush of relief. That was where she was going. He frowned. She had left at noon. If he knew Margarita, she would not want to stop by herself at a posting house. She would probably push to make the whole trip in one day. Nicky was terrible in the carriage, but she would not want to have to deal with him in strange surroundings all by herself. She would go straight through to Winslow.

He felt immensely better, having come to this conclusion. He looked at his watch. He would have light for at least four more hours. He ran downstairs and told Reid to have his curricle brought round to the door in fifteen minutes and to have some cold meat and ale brought to the dining room immediately.

"Yes, my lord," the butler said.

"Her ladyship has gone back to Winslow and I am going to follow her," Nicholas informed him.

"I see, my lord." Reid bowed, his face impassive.

Fifteen minutes later, Nicholas was in his curricle, expertly winding his way through the London streets.

* * *

It was eleven o'clock the following morning when the Earl of Winslow's curricle pulled up at the door of Whitethorn. Emma Frost was in the front yard watering the flowers. "Mr. Nicholas!" she exclaimed, surprise causing her to revert to his old name. She put down her watering can. "I didn't know you were back at Winslow. I hope nothing is wrong?" This last was said a little anxiously, as Nicholas's face was looking alarmingly rigid.

"Is my wife here, Mrs. Frost?" he asked.

The surprise on her face was unquestionably genuine. "Your wife? No. I haven't seen her ladyship since she left for London."

There was no mistaking the shock on Nicholas's face. She saw him shut his eyes. "Are you quite certain?" he then asked, very calmly.

"Yes, my lord." She hesitated. "What has happened?" But the curricle was already moving away, down the well-tended drive.

* * *

They were surprised to see Nicholas at Winslow, but of course, all the servants assumed that Lady Winslow was still in London. If anyone thought it odd that Lord Winslow had arrived alone, without any extra clothing and without his valet, they confined their comments to the servants' quarters. Nicholas went immediately to the library and closed the door behind him. He stood for a very long time looking blindly out the window, his eyes for once focused inward. She was not at Whitethorn. Where, then, could she be? And perhaps even more importantly, why had she gone?

She had left him. Once, long ago, another woman who said she loved him had left him. But he did not feel now, as he had felt then, betrayed and victimized. He knew, had known all along, through all the hours of fast, dangerous driving last night and this morning, that Margarita had not betrayed him. He had betrayed her.

She loved him. He did not question that; he knew it was true. She had fled because she loved him, because it is impossible to live with someone who rejects your love, who holds it carelessly in his hand to be smashed as of no value whenever it becomes inconvenient. Nicholas understood her all too well. Had he not once done the very same thing?

He moved from the window to the worn leather chair and sat down, stretching his legs before him. What a fool he had been, he thought bitterly. What a bloody, infantile fool. "This is not your fault," she had written. As usual, she was being too generous. It was all his fault. Because he was afraid to admit he loved her, he had driven her away. And of course he loved her, had loved her for a long long time. He would give everything he possessed in this world—including Winslow—to get her back.

There was nothing to do but to return to London. She had said she would write him. She must have friends somewhere—possibly South Americans—whom he did not know. The first frantic wave of his fear for her was gone. Margarita was sensible. And she had Nicky with her. No matter how upset she might be, he knew she would never do anything that might possibly harm Nicky. She had said that she had somewhere to go, and he believed her.

He sat on for half an hour longer, and when he rose, it was to go upstairs to his bedroom. He walked over to his wardrobe, slowly took out an old velvet box, and opened it. Inside was a single sheet of paper. He took the paper to the window, and for the first time in seventeen years, he reread the letter his mother had left him when she eloped with John Hamilton.

When he finished, he rested his forehead against the windowpane. From the point of view of a mature, rational mind, the letter was perfectly comprehensible. It was also clear that the writer's heart was very near to breaking.

He closed his eyes and thought back. He knew what his mother's life had been like at Winslow. One of the reasons there was such hostility between him and his uncle was that at a very young age,

Nicholas had constituted himself his mother's protector. His father he remembered only as an occasional brilliant presence, rarely seen and unimportant in his son's life. It was his mother he loved, his mother he learned to fight for and to defend.

And she loved him. For the first time in many years, he allowed himself to remember the warmth and laughter of her, the smile that used to shine out of her eyes whenever their glances chanced to meet. He realized now that his presence had been the only thing that had made life at Winslow bearable to her. And then he went away to school. And John Hamilton arrived. Gentle, sensitive, kind, understanding John Hamilton. Nicholas remembered that once even he had liked the quiet, scholarly man who had stolen his mother.

He looked again at the letter in his hand. "I will always love you," she had written. "They would never let me take you and it would not be right of me to take you. Winslow is your heritage. But I am your mother and I will always love you. Please try to understand. . . ." The words blurred before his eyes. He thought of Margarita having to leave Nicky.

"Poor Mother," he said softly to the quiet air. "What a rotten son you have."

CHAPTER TWENTY-THREE

The heart—the heart—is lonely still.
                                    Byron

When Margarita decided to run away from Nicholas, her biggest problem had been where to go. It was in the hour before dawn that the answer came to her, the one person in England who would have family ties to her, the one place where Nicholas would never look. She went to her mother-in-law.

Charlotte Hamilton lived in a charming cottage near Oxford. Margarita had gotten her direction from Nicholas and written to her after Nicky's birth. They corresponded occasionally since then, both of them carefully avoiding the one name they had in common.

Charlotte and John Hamilton had lived very quietly. He published several histories of medieval England that were well received in academic circles, but he never had a popular success. He lectured at

Oxford, and the money from that, as well as from the articles he wrote for scholarly journals, was what they lived on. Charlotte had been living since his death on the money sent to her quarterly by her son. It was a modest but sufficient sum that allowed her relative comfort for a number of years; she had become accustomed to a limited income. Nicholas increased her allowance considerably when he came into the title and the Winslow collection.

Charlotte was deeply surprised to have Margarita arrive at her front door. She welcomed her daughter-in-law and grandson with brisk kindness, allotted them rooms, sent off to borrow a crib from a neighbor, and saw about dinner. She fed Nicky and helped Margarita put him to bed. Then the two women sat down in the pleasant sitting room and Charlotte said very gently, "Perhaps you had better tell me, my dear."

Margarita looked at Nicholas's mother. Charlotte was in her late forties and looked younger. It would take a shrewd eye to pick out the silver hairs that blended in with the natural blonde of her hair. Her eyes were dark blue and the lines at the corners of them were very faint. She smiled encouragingly at Margarita. "What has Nicholas done?" she asked.

In a low voice, with her eyes on her tensely folded hands, Margarita told her an edited version of the events that brought her to Charlotte's door. The fault, she earnestly insisted, was not Nicholas's. "He was forced to marry me, you see. And he has been so good to me: reading to me when I was sick, teaching me to play cards and to dance, buying me new clothes, and cheering me up when I felt sad. No one could have been kinder. It was not his fault that I fell in love with him. But I did," she said with devastating honesty. "I love him more than anything else in the world, and I cannot bear it that he does not love me."

This was a pain that Charlotte was only too familiar with. Her heart ached for Margarita, and for her son, who would not accept the priceless gift offered to him by his wife. "I needed to be away from him for a little," said Margarita. "To try to understand what it is I must do. May I stay with you? It will only be for a little while." It was a request that Charlotte could not find it in her heart to refuse.

* * *

Margarita sent a message to Nicholas at Berkeley Square, saying that she was safe and with friends and that she did not want to see him yet. She did not give him her direction.

Life at Morgan Cottage soon settled into a routine that revolved largely about the needs of Nicky. Charlotte was thrilled with her grandson and loved to take him out into the garden, where he crawled around on the grass, picking up leaves and worms and flowers. He was tanned and strong and happy and was beginning to drink milk out of a cup.

Margarita, however, was not happy. Her mother-in-law was a kind, undemanding companion, and Margarita was grateful for her quiet understanding and for the sympathy she saw in her dark blue eyes, but somehow, being away from Nicholas did not help. She was even more unhappy than she had been in London. There was a great pit of loneliness deep inside her, and nothing, not Nicky, not Charlotte, could ever serve to fill it up.

She couldn't sleep. She was convinced that she was a failure as a wife and as a mother. She had no patience with Nicky. He tired her unendurably. Charlotte was better with him than she was. His mother had only robbed him of his father and then neglected him herself.

She felt crushingly guilty all the time. She had no right to leave Nicholas. She had gone against the law of God and the law of the land in doing so. And for what reason? Husbands were unfaithful all the time. One week in London had taught her that. Many wives had to put up with far more than she. Nicholas, at least, was only unfaithful when she was out of reach.

She was bitterly, blindingly, unreasoningly jealous of his other women. She knew that. She even knew that she was more important to him than anyone else. But it was not enough.

Suppose I have another child, she thought to herself. Suppose I am sick in bed, for months, as I was with Nicky. How can I bear it, lying there, knowing he is making love to Catherine Alnwick? I cannot bear it. It is impossible.

One week went by and then another. Margarita was thinner, and there were dark smudges under her eyes. "This cannot go on, my dear," Charlotte said to her one night. "You are making yourself ill."

"I know." Margarita looked at her with great, haunted eyes. "I will write and ask Nicholas to come and see me. If he will take me back, I will go."

"You cannot be more unhappy with him than you are here," Charlotte said gently.

"Yes." Margarita gave a slight shrug of her shoulders, and something in that small, resigned movement hurt Charlotte unbearably. She remembered so well what it felt like, to offer love and to have it rejected. She had worshiped brilliant, handsome Christopher Beauchamp when she married him. She could not believe that her son, her Nicholas, was the same kind of man as his father.

"*If* he will take you back?" she said now, carefully.

"Yes." Margarita looked more closely at her face and hastened to add, "Don't look like that, Charlotte. Of course he will take me back. But he will want to—arrange it—so that no one will guess that I ran away. I am sure he has given out some story about my whereabouts that he will want me to support."

Under similar circumstances, Christopher would have taken her back, too, of that Charlotte was certain. But she would have paid for her transgression. She said now to Margarita, "I hope Nicholas won't be too angry."

"He will be angry because he will have been worried about me. But he will forgive me. Nicholas has the unfailing charity of the truly generous."

After Margarita went upstairs to bed, Charlotte sat on for another hour, putting together in her mind all the things she had heard Margarita say of

Nicholas, as if they were a giant puzzle. It seemed to her entirely possible that he was not as indifferent to his wife as Margarita seemed to believe.

The next morning Margarita wrote to Nicholas. She had a reason other than the one she gave Charlotte for wanting him to come to Oxford. She had grown very fond of her mother-in-law and hoped very much for a reconciliation between her husband and his mother. Perhaps if Nicholas came and saw Charlotte, he would relent in his hostility toward her. He might not come. He might just send the coach for her or send her a message. But she thought it was worth a try to get him to Morgan Cottage.

Whatever he wanted her to do, she would do. She had no choice but to go back to him. That was *"la realidad."* She could not stay here forever. Unlike Charlotte, she had no other man to elope with. She could never leave her son, and he was Nicholas's heir; he belonged with his father at Winslow. Duty, convention, the ties of love, all dictated that she return to her husband. She had not spoken to a priest since she left London, but she was in no doubt as to what the Church would tell her. She must go back to Nicholas and try to be a good wife to him. And what Charlotte had said was true: better to be miserable with him than miserable without him. She settled down to fill in the time until she received a response to her letter.

CHAPTER TWENTY-FOUR

> Ah, love, let us be true
> To one another!
> Matthew Arnold

Margarita was correct in assuming that Nicholas had given out a story to explain her sudden absence from Berkeley Square. He told a few hostesses that a Venezuelan friend of hers received news that her brother had been killed at Carúpano, and Margarita went to give what comfort she could to the family. He did not know when to expect her back, he said. He would stay in London until he heard from her.

As he did not want to occasion comment by drastically changing his style of life, he attended a few dinner parties and receptions. He was polite but distant to all his dinner partners; any lady attempting to get up a flirtation with him was rapidly discouraged by the frost in his manner. He did, however, have one encounter with Eleanor Rushton that could not be accurately described as frosty. She came up to him at a crowded reception and put a light hand on his arm. He turned, looked down, and when he saw who it was his eyes narrowed. She took one look at his taut, hostile, contemptuous face and removed her hand as if it suddenly burned. "You have done your damage," he said in a low voice that seemed to cut through to the bone. "I never want to see you again."

"Nicholas!" she said pleadingly, but the bitter, ruthless line of his mouth did not relax. He turned and left her. She did not go near him again.

* * *

He was in London for over two weeks before Margarita's second letter came. The relief he felt when he saw her small, precise handwriting on the envelope was so intense that he had to close his eyes for a minute. He was by himself in the breakfast room and he carefully slit the envelope and extracted the letter. He read:

Morgan Cottage
August, 1816

My Lord,
If you will take me back I am ready to come. I have been staying here at Morgan Cottage with your mother for these last weeks. She has been so kind to me and to Nicky. Please do not be angry with her for not telling you of my whereabouts. I promised her faithfully that I would do that myself.

It was wicked of me to have run away. I know you must have been worried and I am sorry. I will try very hard to be a good wife to you in the future.

I would like it very much if you would come to Morgan Cottage to get me. If you feel you cannot, I shall understand. I will do whatever you want me to.

Your wife,
Margarita Beauchamp

Nicholas finished the letter and then reread it. Margarita spoke excellent English but was less comfortable writing it. Nevertheless, something in the simple, almost childlike, sentences hurt him savagely. With his mouth set in a severe line, he looked again at the opening sentence. So that was where she had gone. He knew she corresponded with his mother. He didn't know why he hadn't thought of that possibility before.

He rang the bell, and when Reid appeared he began to issue orders. "I shall be escorting her ladyship and Lord Seldon back to Winslow, Reid. I want a bag packed for me immediately. Have the carriage at the door in forty-five minutes, please. I also want Mrs. Wade, her ladyship's personal maid, and my valet to return to Winslow today. I will be taking the carriage so you will need to hire a post chaise for them. See to it, will you?"

"Yes, my lord," said Reid. He was almost smiling. Nicholas went upstairs to dress and in forty-five minutes was on his way to Oxford.

* * *

It was a beautiful, warm summer day when the Earl of Winslow's carriage stopped in front of a charming brick cottage with a front yard full of truly magnificent flowers. He told the coachman to take the horses to an inn in Oxford and wait for further directions. The carriage pulled away and he was left looking at his mother's house. Very slowly, he walked up the path.

His knock was answered by a young maidservant, who showed him into a cozy sunny room with faded chintz and bowls of flowers. Mrs. Hamilton was in the garden, she told him. Whom should she say was asking to see her?

"The Earl of Winslow," said Nicholas.

The young girl's eyes widened, and she left the room with rapid steps. After her footsteps faded, the house was quiet. Nicholas listened, but could hear no sound of either his wife or his son. He walked to the window and looked out at a beautiful rose garden. He was still standing there, looking at the garden, when his mother came to the door. The maid had not closed it, and he did not hear the light step on the worn carpeting, but quite suddenly he knew she was there. He had always known, he remembered, whenever she entered a room he was in. He turned around. "Hello, Mother," he said.

Her hair was less silver than gold, he saw, and her eyes were the same vivid dark blue. He would know those eyes anywhere. She was very pale, but at his words the color flushed into her cheeks, making her look almost as young as he remembered her. She looked, searchingly, into his face. "Nicholas," she said falteringly, and then, hesitantly held out her hands. He was across the room in two strides and had her in his arms.

Charlotte was the one to loosen her grip first. "Let me look at you," she said softly, and reached up to cup his face between her hands. "You've grown so tall! Why you must be over six feet."

"Six-three, to be precise," he answered, smiling down at her. "It annoyed my uncle no end that he had to look up at me."

"You get your height from the Holts," she said. She turned him a little toward the window so the sun fell full on his face, then she let him go. "You're even better looking than your father, and I always thought he was the most handsome man I had ever seen."

"I seem to have inherited more than his looks," Nicholas said, a strain of bitterness in his voice. "Can you ever forgive me, Mother, for my abominable behavior toward you all these years?"

"There is nothing to forgive," she replied calmly. "I always understood how you felt."

A muscle jumped along his jaw. "God!" he exclaimed. "The generosity of women! I totally ignore my mother for seventeen years and she says there's nothing to forgive. I behave so outrageously to my wife that she is forced to flee from my house, and then she writes to tell me it was wicked of her to leave me, that she will try to be a good wife to me in the future, and will I please take her back. The both of you ought to tell me never to darken your doors again."

Charlotte was smiling at him. She picked up his hand and patted it. "We could never do that. Now tell me, *do* you want Margarita back?"

He stared at her. "Want her back? Of course I want her back!"

"Why, Nicholas?"

Her eyes, with the glimmer of a smile in the dark blue depths, were so familiar. "Because I love her," he replied, his voice calmer than it had been.

The smile in her eyes grew. "I thought perhaps you might. She has been so very unhappy, Nicholas."

"I know. This whole mess has been my fault, Mother. I only hope I can put it right."

"Just tell her what you told me, darling. That is what she needs to hear."

Her eyes held his for a minute longer and then he sighed. "Yes, I know. Where is she now?"

"She went up to her room to lie down."

He hesitated a minute and she said, "It is the second door on the right as you go down the hallway. Go up to her, Nicholas."

"Thank you, Mother," he said simply, and went.

* * *

It was a warm day and Margarita had taken off her dress and lain down in her chemise and petticoat. She was lying curled on her side, trying to stop thinking and drift off to sleep, when a knock came at the door. Startled, she sat up. "Yes?" she called. "Is it you, Charlotte? Come in." The door opened and her husband was there.

"It isn't Charlotte," he said. "May I come in?"

"Nicholas!" Her hand flew to her throat. "Yes, of course. Come in. I did not think to see you so quickly."

"Did you not?" He closed the door behind him and came over to the bed. "My mother sent me up," he said.

"Your mother? Oh, Nicholas, have you seen her then?"

"Yes. And I have apologized for my outrageous neglect, and she has assured me that I am forgiven."

"I am so glad," she said softly.

He stood silent for a minute, gathering his thoughts and looking at her. "Will *you* forgive me?" he asked.

She bowed her head. "It is I who should be asking that of you. It was very wrong of me to have run away."

"It was the smartest thing you could have done," he said flatly, and she raised wide, wondering eyes to his face. It was very serious. "I have loved you for so long, Margarita, but it wasn't until you left me that I realized how very much you meant to me. You are the most important thing in the world to me, and I will never ever even look at another woman again. I promise."

At his first mention of love, Margarita's eyes began to glow, and by the time his speech was finished her face was radiant. "Oh, Nicholas," she said huskily. "Oh, my love." Then she was in his arms, the roughness of his coat under her cheek. She closed her eyes and clung to him tightly. His cheek was against her hair.

"My little love," he was saying. "My little love." Then, his voice sounding rougher, he said, "I meant what I said just now, Margarita. I only got involved with those other women because I was trying to prove to myself that I didn't need you. It was a piece of colossal stupidity only I could have invented. And all I succeeded in doing was demonstrating the opposite."

Her voice was muffled by his shoulder. "You don't have to explain."

He put his hands on her shoulders and held her away from him. "Are you going to let me get off scot-free, then?" he asked softly.

The brown eyes gazing at him were big and dark and bottomless. "Yes," she whispered.

His face was intent, profoundly serious. She knew what was coming next and felt the tremor deep within her. She raised her face a little, and his mouth came down on top of hers.

* * *

"We'll go back to Winslow," he said about an hour later. "You don't really like London, and Nicky is much better off in the country."

She smiled. "I do like it best at Winslow. I have you and I have Nicky. I don't need anything else."

"Mmm." He was propped on one elbow, looking down at her face.

"Perhaps we can have another baby," she said, very softly.

"That would be nice, but I wouldn't mind waiting for a little while." Very gently he ran his finger around her nipple. "Trying to make one is so much fun."

"Nicholas . . ." She tried to ignore the ache inside her his roving finger was creating. "What must your mother be thinking?"

"The worst," he murmured, and after a moment of token resistance, she capitulated.

They missed tea and arrived downstairs only five minutes before dinner. "Nicky has been fed and is now asleep," Charlotte informed them placidly. She looked shrewdly at the two young faces before her and smiled. "Dinner is served. You must be hungry."

Nicholas grinned. "Starved, Mother," he said, and Margarita blushed.

Later, after dinner, as they sat in the comfortable sitting room, he said, "Would you care to come and live at Winslow, Mother? Both Margarita and I would love to have you."

There was suspicious brightness in Charlotte's eyes, but she shook her head. "Thank you, darling, but I like my little cottage. It holds many happy memories for me, and I have some good friends in the neighborhood. When John died, I was afraid I should have to give it up, but thanks to my son I was able to keep it."

"You owe small thanks to your son for anything, Mother," he said bitterly.

Charlotte smiled at Margarita. "For how long do you think he means to keep this up?"

Margarita's answering smile was full of identical humor and tolerance. "I don't know," she replied.

Nicholas scanned their two faces, taking in the kinship of expression. "Not for very long if you two plan to take sides against me," he said drily, and both his mother and his wife laughed.

"But seriously, Charlotte," Margarita said, "if you won't make your home with us, I hope you will come on long visits. Nicky has grown so fond of you. And I, also."

Charlotte smiled. "And I have come to love you both."

"Then you will at least come for visits?" put in Nicholas.

"You couldn't keep me away," she assured him. She was sitting in a high-backed chintz-covered chair, her hands resting loosely on the arms. Nicholas leaned forward a little from the sofa where he was seated next to Margarita, and briefly covered one of his mother's hands with his own. She looked for a minute at the large, strong hand that rested on hers and then raised her eyes to his face. The gray-green eyes were warm and unguarded, and reflected back her own feelings of tenderness and love.

"We will expect you next week, then," said Margarita serenely.

Nicholas removed his hand from his mother's and turned to look at his wife. He had a sudden urge to put his arm around her and hold her to him. All this, he thought, his mind encompassing Charlotte, the warmth and love in the room, the baby sleeping upstairs, all of this is because of Margarita. But he refrained from reaching for her; her Spanish dignity would be offended by so public an embrace. He contented himself with an endorsement of her invitation. "Next week," he repeated, then yawned hugely. "By George, but I'm tired. Think I'll turn in."

His mother looked amused. "By all means. It has been a rather exciting day. You two go ahead upstairs. I'll just see about locking up here below."

"Good night, Mother." He bent and kissed her cheek. He went to the door and held it for his wife. "Coming, Margarita?"

"Good night, Charlotte," she said sedately. She too kissed her mother-in-law's cheek and then crossed the room to her husband. With beautiful dignity, she passed out of the room, and Nicholas, watching her straight back as it preceded him up the stairs, smiled imperceptibly.